I was inside the ali

I hauled myself silently out of the air shaft and into the control room. Staying in a half crouch, I crept up on the hideous alien manning the computer. I was hoping I could knock him unconscious.

But then I saw something on his monitor that froze my blood in its veins.

It was a picture of me. A live video image.

With words underneath it:

TARGET: JACK RAYNES
LOCATION: METIER, WISCONSIN
ORDERS: SEEK AND DESTROY

"No!" I screamed, too late. Before I could react, a clear plastic tube shot down from the ceiling, encasing me.

I'd walked straight into a trap!

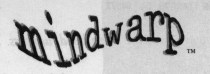
mindwarp™

Alien Terror
Alien Blood
Alien Scream

Available from MINSTREL® Paperbacks

mindwarp ™

Alien Scream

by

Chris Archer

A MINSTREL® BOOK

Published by POCKET BOOKS

New York   London   Toronto   Sydney   Tokyo   Singapore

A MINSTREL PAPERBACK *Original*

A Minstrel Book published by
POCKET BOOKS, a division of Simon & Schuster Inc.
1230 Avenue of the Americas, New York, NY 10020

mindwarp™ is a trademark of Daniel Weiss Associates, Inc.
Produced by Daniel Weiss Associates, Inc., New York

ISBN: 0-671-01484-6

First Minstrel Books printing December 1997

10 9 8 7 6 5 4 3 2 1

Printed in the U.S.A.

For Craig

Alien Scream

Chapter 1

It was almost go time. The alien base was only a few miles off. We were nearly there.

I looked out the truck window for the hundredth time at the devastated remains of my hometown. One of the charred buildings was still smoldering, even though the alien attack had taken place over a month ago. With a shock, I realized that the blackened shell had once been the town's fire station.

I remembered being taken there after the Labor Day parade. I remembered how the cherry red fire trucks gleamed in the sunlight, how the firemen smiled and waved.

It was all gone. Destroyed. They had taken it from us.

Now it was payback time.

Metier, Wisconsin, was ground zero in the battle for the fate of the human race.

I turned my gaze from the window.

There were thirteen of us in the truck, thirteen battle-hardened killing machines, an elite force called Alpha Platoon. It was hard to believe that only a few weeks ago, we were just thirteen seventh-graders at Metier Junior High. Now, instead of staying up late doing our homework, we were staying up late studying battle plans.

Leave it to interplanetary warfare to ruin your childhood.

A.J., the company commander, barked orders at us while jabbing a pointer at a diagram of a "bug" flickering on the enormous computer monitor they'd rigged up inside the truck.

That was the nickname we'd given the aliens: *bugs*.

It was the way they looked: gray, featureless skin, little slits for mouths, and—where their eyes were supposed to be—two big black disks that seemed to suck in the light.

And it was the way they attacked. The Australian dragonfly, the world's fastest insect, can reach speeds of up to 36 miles per hour. The alien bugs struck our little town at a hundred times that speed. They descended at dawn like a cloud of locusts, destroying every bridge, road, and building in a matter of minutes. From Metier, the swarm went on to Chicago, New York, and Washington, D.C.

By nightfall, our planet was under their control.

The worst part was that we had seen the signs, but we had chosen to ignore them.

Metier had always had a reputation as a hot spot for alien sightings. Some people even called it the "Roswell of the North." For years, campers, hikers, and truck drivers had come into town telling of the strange lights they'd seen over our reservoir. It had gotten so bad that the police stopped responding to the reports. They said it was all imaginary nonsense.

If only they'd taken it seriously. If only they'd sent a search team to the heart of the woods around the reservoir. If only they'd found the huge, humming metal structure with the strange markings on its side. If only they'd destroyed the alien base before the bugs landed and launched their devastating attack.

But they hadn't. And now we were going to have to do it the hard way.

Our mission was crazy and desperate, but we were living in crazy, desperate times. The human race was about to lose the game. Alpha Platoon was its last hope—thirteen kids who could sneak into the alien headquarters, plant a pulse detonator, and set it off.

Of course, they'd given us an escape plan, but we knew that we'd never get a chance to use it. This was our last mission: Do or die.

A.J. droned on and on about strategy and

vulnerable points as the truck rumbled over the pock-marked dirt road. I was still staring at the diagram of the bug glowing on the computer screen. That horrible face.

How do you wait until you see the whites of their eyes, I thought, *when there* aren't *any whites in their eyes?*

Suddenly, the truck's huge twin-V engines ground to a halt. We were there.

It was go time.

The next thing I knew, I was dashing across the concrete apron of the reservoir toward the forest ahead. This was the deadliest part of the mission: Between the truck and the safety of the woods, there was no cover. The thin blue vapor from our smoke screen offered minimal protection. If any of the bugs decided they were in the mood for target practice, we were wide open.

My feet pounded against the firm concrete. My pulse pounded against my eardrums. The acrid blue smoke burned my nostrils and tore at the back of my throat. The shelter of the woods was getting closer, but I wasn't there yet. The muscles in my legs screamed at me, strained past their limit. I ignored them and ran on.

Suddenly, thin needlepoints of red light flashed around me: alien fire! They were shooting at us! I saw two of Alpha Platoon's best soldiers hit the ground and roll.

For the tenth time, I wished that I had a weapon. But I had a bigger responsibility—setting the pulse detonator. As A.J. pointed out, a weapon was excess baggage that would only have slowed me down. I ran zigzag, hoping to make myself a more difficult target.

Finally, my breath coming in ragged gasps, I burst through the tree line. Laser fire *pinged* futilely against the sheltering trees. Alpha Platoon's enrollment had been reduced from thirteen to eight. And we weren't even at the hard part yet. The alien base still loomed ahead, like a humming metal tomb.

The tunnel was right where the blueprints said it would be, a service conduit running from the edge of the reservoir straight beneath the alien base. Still running at top speed, I threw myself down the entrance ramp that led into the tunnel, bouncing on my butt as I went.

The gluteus maximus, or buttock, is the largest muscle in the human body, weighing approximately eight pounds on a teenage male. After skidding down that hard concrete, I figured I had only about three pounds left. Five had died.

Soon, I was crawling on my hands and knees through the darkness of the tunnel. Behind me, A.J. was hollering, *"Go, go, go!"* My heart was pounding so loudly, I could barely hear him. Then, without warning, A.J. stopped yelling.

He'd been neutralized.

No more A.J.

I couldn't think about that. I had a planet to save.

I was looking for an air vent, a shaft that led upward from the tunnel into the alien control room. At the final mission meeting, we had been told to look for a red X that marked the shaft's position. But it was too dark to see! What if I had already passed it? What if I lost myself in the tunnels under the alien base and never got out again?

Just as I was starting to panic, I heard a hollow metal *clang* above me: the sound of movement overhead. The shaft had to be close by. Then I saw the X at my feet, half hidden by the swirling blue smoke. I looked up. The hatch was above me—just a square panel in the tunnel's ceiling. I put my shoulder against it and pushed. Silently, it opened upward.

I peered around. The room the shaft opened into held dazzling arrays of computer circuitry, row after row of elaborate controls, and the thick glass "eggs" the bugs had used to flatten New York, Los Angeles, and Tokyo. It was the control room, all right.

Jackpot.

I patted the pulse detonator in its long, tubular holster. "C'mon baby," I said. "Time to do a little bug zapping."

But something was bothering me. What had made

the sound I heard? Had it been a footstep? My brain was shouting at me: *Be careful, Jack.*

With no warning, a bug soldier entered the room, walking quickly to one of the complex terminals. I ducked out of sight before he saw me. I braced my back against the wall of the shaft, held my breath, and waited.

What was I going to do? What was I going to do? The I-wish-I-had-a-weapon count hit eleven. I wondered if I could put the bug in a tiger hold and knock him unconscious. That was my only hope.

As quietly as possible, I hauled myself out of the shaft and into the control room. Staying in a half crouch, I crept up on my unsuspecting insectoid victim. I stood up behind him, readying myself for the lightning strike.

But then I saw something on his monitor that froze my blood in its veins.

It was a picture of me. A live video image.

With words underneath it.

TARGET: JACK RAYNES
LOCATION: METIER, WISCONSIN
ORDERS: SEEK AND DESTROY

"No!" I screamed, realizing I'd walked straight into a trap. But I was too late. Before I could react, a clear plastic tube shot down from the ceiling, encasing me. My hands were pinned to my sides!

I struggled against the tight plastic prison. I couldn't save myself, but I could still complete my mission. If I could just set off the pulse detonator, if I could just reach my holster . . .

The bug spun to face me. "Jack Raynes," it said, grinning sinisterly. "Seek and destroy."

The tallest man in history had an arm span of nine feet, five and three-quarter inches. If only mine were half of that!

My fingertips brushed the edge of the detonator. I strained to access the flat trigger panel by my knee, to press the neon yellow button that would end this nightmare. I wriggled desperately, trying to jam my arm further down. A few seconds were all that I needed—

But it was more time than I had.

"Jack Raynes," the bug said again, pointing a torque blaster at my forehead. "Found and . . . *eliminated.*"

He fired—

And then the world went red.

In big, glowing block letters, the words inside my plastic laser-tag helmet read:

STATUS: FATAL HIT
GAME OVER

And the worst part is, I was out of tokens.

8

Chapter 2

I met up with the rest of the "eliminated" Alpha Platoon in the food court, in front of the Pizza Palace.

A triple-decker deluxe was waiting at our table—that's where they sandwich a jumbo pizza between two other jumbo pizzas. It wasn't the largest pizza in the world (which had a diameter of 122 feet and took over 100 gallons of sauce and a ton of mozzarella cheese to make), but I'm pretty sure it was the largest pizza ever to have the words "Happy 13th Birthday, Jack" spelled out in pepperoni.

I took my seat at the head of the table.

My fellow "soldiers" and I fall several hundred notches on the coolness scale when we make the transition from the virtual world to the real one. I suppose you could say we're in that awkward stage.

I, for one, have horrible reddish hair, a face plagued by the more-than-occasional zit, and a voice that can jump without warning from a deep baritone to a pitch only a ventriloquist dummy could be proud of. To top it off, my mom won't buy or let me do anything that even vaguely threatens to be cool. The only reason she let me hang at the mall tonight, a school night, was because it was my birthday.

I was waiting to find out what my best friend, Cleveland, had to say about Aliencounter, the laser-tag game we'd just played. I suppose Aliencounter is the first truly cool thing to ever happen in our town: an actual game based on the place we grew up in.

It was bound to happen. Like I said, people really do call us the "Roswell of the North." The town's name, Metier, even looks like *meteor*, which is what everyone calls it, though it's supposed to be pronounced "met-ee-ay." I think it's French or something. I was never good with languages.

In fact, I'm not good at much of anything they teach at Metier Junior High. My mom says I'm an underachiever. *I* say I'm under*interested*.

I spend most of the school day just trying to stay awake, and the rest of it failing to. The only thing I like about school is that the library holds every edition of *The Guinness Book of Records* going back to the very first one in 1956.

It's my goal to get my name in there some day. I'm not sure what for, but I know it will happen—I just gotta find my unique talent.

For a couple weeks this summer I tried growing the world's longest fingernails, but my mom put a stop to my attempt 250 inches short of the record 251. When I told her she had heartlessly clipped away my dreams, she said I should forget about fingernails and instead try setting the record for World's Most Obedient Son.

She's a laugh riot, my mom is.

Cleveland, on the other hand, is kind of an authority on video games. In case you're wondering, his real name isn't Cleveland. It's Michael. He got his nickname because he wears a big hat like Indiana Jones wore in *Raiders of the Lost Ark.* He thought it would make him look bigger—he's only four foot five—but if you ask me, it kind of backfired. When he first started wearing it, somebody said there wasn't enough of him to make an Indiana, but maybe he could be a Cleveland. And the name stuck.

Cleveland put down his Massive Blast—sixty-four ounces of pure cola pleasure, and almost as big as he is—and looked around the table, ready to make his pronouncement.

The feasting halted. The table went silent.

"It didn't suck," Cleveland finally said.

We all nodded and resumed chewing. From Cleveland, this was high praise.

"Cool weapons," I weighed in.

"Cool VR effects," Ben Jameson said.

"Cool sounds," Nick Carlucci added.

"The sounds were lame," Vinnie Carlucci cut in. "But the fake smoke was cool." Nick and Vinnie were twins. They hated each other, but they went everywhere together.

"Shut up, butt-mouth," Nick told Vinnie.

"You shut up, butt-mouth*ette*," Vinnie told Nick.

I guess some people are just gluttons for punishment.

"What about those stupid-looking aliens?" said Byron Prendergast.

And other people are just gluttons.

Byron was stuffing the remains of his second slice into his mouth and reaching for a third. It's hard to realize how impressive this feat is until you take into account that each slice of a triple-decker deluxe weighs in at close to a pound. "Come on—how many times have these guys seen *Close Encounters of the Third Kind?*"

"Maybe that's just what aliens look like," said Leonard Dooley, shrugging. Leonard was a good guy, but not the sharpest tool in the shed. He sometimes had a hard time telling the difference between fact and fantasy.

"Leonard," Byron said over a mouthful of pizza, "there's no such thing as aliens. Remember?"

"Oh . . . right," Leonard said.

12

"How do you know there aren't any aliens?" I was about to ask, when suddenly my throat closed off, my heart stopped dead, and the room started spinning.

I couldn't breathe. I couldn't move. I wondered how much longer I had before I passed out.

There, not twenty feet away, stood Jenny Kim and Ashley Rose. The two girls were buying frozen lemonades at the corn-dog booth. So far they hadn't noticed our table.

This was a good thing.

Cleveland poked me in the ribs. "Hey, Jack," he teased, "it's your girlfriend."

"Shut up!" I whispered through clenched teeth. "I do *not* like Jenny Kim."

And I don't. Not exactly.

I mean, I do kind of get a funny feeling when she's around, like I might be dying from lack of oxygen. But that's to be expected.

Let's face it, if there was a *Guinness Book of Records* just for Metier, Wisconsin, Jenny Kim would be listed as Funniest, Happiest, and Prettiest.

Ashley, on the other hand, would get Most Disturbed.

For one thing, Ashley's one of those kids who wears only black, as if her life's a great big funeral. For another, last month she fell through the ice on the town reservoir and nearly drowned.

13

She says she was being chased, but no one in school believes her. They think she, like, *wanted* to fall in the water. As a joke, some kids even started calling her "Splashley Rose" and "Ashley Sunk" behind her back.

I guess you gotta expect it when you dress like a member of the Addams Family.

Of course, Jenny Kim believes Ashley's story. But that's what best friends are supposed to do.

Heck, I thought, *if Cleveland told some nutso tale that everybody doubted, I'd stick by his side, too.*

"Who said anything about Jenny?" Cleveland said, shooting the rest of the table a wicked grin. "I was talking about Ashley Rose."

Then again, maybe I wouldn't.

Byron Prendergast laughed really loudly, spewing tomato sauce down his double chin. This made everyone else at the table crack up.

Jenny looked over and spotted us. She waved.

Oh no, I thought, staring down at my plate. *Please, don't let her come over here. Please, please, please—*

By the third *please,* Jenny was standing in front of me. Ashley Rose stood beside her, looking creepy in her black hooded ski parka. She sucked noisily at her lemonade.

"Hey, Jack," Jenny said. She cast an eye on the rapidly disintegrating pizza. By this time it read, "py 3th hday ack." "Is it your birthday?" she inquired.

14

I didn't know what to say.

"Say 'yes,'" Cleveland whispered in my ear.

"Yes!" I said loudly. "Yes, it, uh, is my birthday. Yes."

Like I said, I'm not too good with languages, and whenever Jenny Kim is around, that includes English.

"So," Jenny said. "How's it feel to be a big old teenager?"

She smiled, fixing me in her pretty brown-eyed gaze. I was momentarily fascinated by the dimple in her chin, at the way her nose crinkled.

Then Cleveland kicked my shin under the table.

"Oh! Um. Not bad," I stammered. "I mean, uh, pretty great, actually, considering I just spent the last hour battling bug-eyed aliens."

My lame attempt at conversation was totally destroyed as Ashley Rose spat an entire mouthful of lemon slush in my face.

"*What?*" Ashley croaked, looking kind of bug-eyed herself.

"We just played Aliencounter," I said, reaching for the napkin dispenser. I wiped my dripping cheeks and brow.

Geez. What did she *think* I said? "Please put out the fire on my forehead"?

Ashley blinked, then shook her head. "Oh . . . right," she said, sounding oddly relieved. "I mean . . .

15

Aliencounter," she continued. "I, uh, got to check that out."

For a second, nobody said anything, but we were all thinking the same thing: *Falling through the ice really messes you up.*

"Well, we're on our way to the movies," Jenny chimed in, a tad too brightly. She glanced at her watch. "Correction: We're *late* for the movies. Gotta go." She grabbed Ashley's hand. "Have a happy birthday, Jack."

"Thanks," I replied as Jenny led Ashley away. "You too."

"'You too'?" Cleveland said later, when we were paid up and headed out of the mall. "Jenny's birthday isn't till June!"

"I know," I mumbled. "I just got . . . confused."

Cleveland stopped walking and crossed his arms. He stared at me, shaking his head slowly. "Boy, are you a wuss, Raynes."

"How am I a wuss?" I demanded.

"Because you totally want to ask Jenny Kim out, and every time you get a chance, you whiff."

"I don't want to ask her out," I said.

"*Sure* you don't," Cleveland said. "That's why you do your Incredible Stuttering Man impression every time she comes by: 'Um, uh, hi, ah, um, uh, J-J-Jenny.'"

I would have argued with him, but he had a point.

16

"I'll tell you what," Cleveland said. He poked his thumb into his chest. *"I'm* going to help you out."

"How?" I asked warily.

"I'm going to ask her out for you." Smiling smugly, he started heading toward the mall exit.

"What?" I yelled after him. "Cleveland, I do *not* like her!"

"Jack," he said, turning around. "You are ruining your reputation, and since I'm your best friend, you are ruining mine. I'll give you until the end of school tomorrow. If you don't do it by then . . . I'm doing it for you."

I looked into his eyes. He meant it.

"Besides," he continued, "what's the worst that could happen?"

It was a crazy and desperate mission, but I was living in crazy, desperate times. I had twenty-four hours. Twenty-four hours to save my own life.

I was so wrapped up in my thoughts that I didn't hear the screams until it was too late.

Chapter 3

"Stay calm!" the police officer yelled as he ran through the mall. "Everybody just stay calm! Nothing to get excited about!"

If ever there was a sign that there's something to be excited about, it's an officer of the law running and yelling that there's nothing to be excited about.

Shoppers shrank back against the walls. Mothers clutched their small children protectively. The policeman was headed toward the Aliencounter area.

Cleveland looked at me and I looked at him.

"Cool!" we said at the same time and dashed toward the laser arcade.

A small crowd had gathered outside the Aliencounter entrance to watch the commotion. Cleveland and I pushed our way to the front.

I didn't know what I thought I'd see. Had the laser guns started a fire? Did some teenager flip out and get stuck inside the tunnels? But what I actually saw was stranger than anything I could have imagined.

There, standing on the counter where you buy tokens, was what looked like an oversized nine-volt battery pointing a bow and arrow at three bug-eyed aliens cowering on the floor.

The aliens, of course, were just Aliencounter workers—the people who own it made them dress up in big rubber costumes, complete with tentacles. Pretty humiliating, if you ask me.

The giant battery was Ed Beister, better known to residents of Metier as Mister Transistor.

Ed Beister is a pretty strange sight: He has aluminum foil taped over all of his clothes, so he looks like a big, walking baked potato. Plus he wears this kind of antenna hat on his head. The old guy seems to live in the mall. My mom said he used to be a pretty famous lawyer and then one day—boom—he just snapped. No one knows why.

The bow in Ed's hands still had a tag dangling from it that said "Hargrove's," our local sporting goods store. I could see big Mr. Hargrove standing in the crowd, being held back by the police.

Cleveland leaned toward me. "Who does old Beister think he's holding up with that bow and arrow," he whispered in my ear. "Bambi?"

Ed was in rare form. "Don't you see, people?" he hollered at the crowd. "They're aliens! And they're all around us! Your lives are in danger!"

Someone from the crowd piped up, "I think *you're* the only alien here, Ed."

Everyone laughed.

"They're just kids in costumes, Ed," said a tall police officer with short brown hair. He was speaking softly and calmly, like you would to a spooked horse. "Drop the bow and put your hands on your head." There were four officers now, but none of them looked very worried.

"I'm trying to save your life!" Ed howled, pointing the arrow at the "aliens." "I'm trying to save all of you! They're aaaaliens!"

"Ed," said the tall officer, a little more forcibly. "Drop that weapon or I'll have to come in there after you. You don't want that, do you?"

With a little moan, Ed let the bow drop from his fingers. "I tried to warn you," he sobbed. "I really tried."

"Okay, let's go. You know the drill." The police officers fanned out around Ed, taking him gently by the arms.

"Where are you taking him, Chief Rogers?" asked one of the Aliencounter workers, her antennae bobbing as she got up off the floor.

"This is strike three for Ed," said the tall policeman. "It's time he paid a visit to the county jail."

The officers led Ed Beister away from the token booth. For the first time, I started to feel bad for him. It must be hard to have to live in a mall. His head was down and he looked like my neighbor's dog, Roxie, after a scolding.

But as the police procession passed me and Cleveland, Ed suddenly perked up. He froze in his tracks, snapping his head toward me. *"You!"* he shouted, staring directly into my eyes.

I was startled. "Me?" I squeaked.

"Come on, Ed! What's the matter with you?" Chief Rogers said.

But Ed's hand shot out, grabbing hold of my jacket. "Your life is in danger!" he shouted. "Save yourself!"

"That's it, Ed," Chief Rogers said. "Time to go."

The officers pried Ed Beister away from me, then dragged him out the exit.

I just stood there, weirded out.

"Wow," Cleveland said. "Happy Birthday from Planet Odd."

I didn't think anything of Ed's warning at the time.

It wasn't until the next morning that I found the note.

The note in my hands was exactly one sentence long.

"Your life is in danger." That was all it said.

Someone had slipped it into my coat pocket. I had no idea who.

I looked around the school yard in both directions.

There was no one watching me, no one looking to see if I got it, no one waiting to check my reaction, no one special at all. Just the usual group of kids milling around the courtyard, waiting for the early bell to ring.

If it were any other day, I might have spent more time trying to figure out what the note meant and where it had come from. But that morning I had no time for stupid pranks. That morning, I, Jack Raynes, was on a mission.

So without a moment's hesitation, I crumpled the note into a ball and threw it into the big wire trash can next to the entrance. Or, anyway, I threw it *at* the trash can next to the entrance—it bounced off the rim and fell to the ground. Athletics has never been my strong point.

Turning from the trash can, my eyes swept the courtyard. It wasn't long before they landed on my target. And stuck there.

Let me tell you a little bit more about the natural marvel that is Jenny Kim. Jenny has short dark hair, a really great face, and she's trim from being on the swim team. One reason I think Jenny's so cool is that she wasn't born in Metier. She was born in Seoul, which is in Korea.

And Jenny is *not* a lip gloss and nail polish kind of girl. Far from it. That morning, Jenny was playing Whip-It on the brick wall by the cafeteria. She was playing a bunch of guys on the soccer team for their lunch money.

Cleveland was waiting for me under the basketball hoop.

"Hey, Jack," he said when he saw me. "It's go time."

Once Cleveland gets it into his head to do something, he does it. And if he asked Jenny Kim out for me, it would be ten times as embarrassing as doing it myself.

So this was it. My last chance.

A suicide mission.

Of course, they'd given us an escape plan.

"This is dumb," I protested. "I don't even like her!"

"Oh yeah? Then what are you trying to do when you always stare at her—read the brand name on her retainer?" He paused, then went on. "Come on, Jack. What's the worst thing that could happen?"

"She could laugh at me," I said. "And her friends could laugh at me, and the guys she's playing handball with could laugh at me, and in my seventh-grade yearbook I could be remembered as the guy who Jenny Kim laughed at."

"Okay," Cleveland shot back. "Then what's the best thing that could happen? She says 'yes,' and you take her out to a movie, and then you start going on dates. And in your seventh-grade yearbook you're the guy who took Jenny Kim to the prom."

I looked at Jenny. She had just finished a match with Jeff Galries, the soccer team's star forward. It looked as if Jeff wasn't going to be eating lunch today. He was slumped over the bench, panting.

Jenny had barely broken a sweat.

I tried picturing her in a prom dress, standing at my side.

It was worth the humiliation.

"Okay," I said. "I'll do it."

Even then, I knew that something strange was going on. I felt sick. Not an I-don't-want-to-make-an-idiot-out-of-myself-in-front-of-this-girl kind of sick. Sick, as in actually sick. But a moment later, there I was, walking across the blacktop. It was a struggle just to put one foot in front of the other. But somehow I managed.

Before I knew it, I was standing next to her.

I looked back at Cleveland. He gave me the thumbs-up signal. I was so dizzy at this point, it looked as if there were three Clevelands, each in an identical hat.

Jenny looked at me and smiled. I noticed that she had a very big, very white smile. "Hi," she said, blowing a strand of hair out of her eyes. "You want winners?"

"Sure," I said.

Then suddenly something hit me hard in the side of the head. I pitched forward onto the pavement, and the world went black.

Chapter 4

When I came to, Drew Molinari was standing over me, tossing a baseball from hand to hand.

Drew is the star of the wrestling team. Drew is not particularly smart in much the same way that the Pacific Ocean is not particularly dry. Jenny was standing right next to him, looking down at me in amazement.

I had landed on my back on the pavement.

The next time Cleveland asks me, "What's the worst that could happen?" I thought, *I'll have to remember this moment.*

"Hey, Raynes," Drew sneered. "Watch where you're standing. Your big head got in the way of my throw."

"Shut up, you creep," Jenny said. "The way you throw, I'm surprised he even felt it."

Great, I thought. *Jenny is going to fight Drew for me.*

Just then, Mr. Eggleston, the assistant principal,

came over. His look of concern changed to one of suspicion when he saw who it was lying on the pavement.

When you have forty-one tardies in a given academic year, teachers tend not to trust you.

"All right. What happened?" he asked.

"Drew pegged him in the back of the head with a baseball," Jenny said.

Mr. Eggleston bent down. "Jack, are you okay?" he asked. "How many fingers?"

Counting has never been a problem for me. I bet Drew wishes he could say the same. "Three," I said weakly.

Mr. Eggleston frowned. "You'd better go to the nurse. Jenny, can you take him there?"

"Sure," she said. Then she held out her hand to me.

I may have been lying down, but things were definitely looking *up*.

"What was that like?" Jenny wanted to know as we pushed through the double doors into the stuffy air of the school building. The bell for homeroom had just rung. The hall was packed with other kids, all busy at their lockers.

"What?"

"Passing out."

"Uh . . ." *Think, Jack, think.* "It was kind of, like, wham. Suddenly you're, like, going to sleep, but, uh, really fast." *Brilliant. Superb. You are a master of the English language.*

"It was pretty cool to watch you," Jenny said. "Your head rolled back, then your knees folded. It was like a building going down."

"Oh, I get knocked out all the time," I said, trying to sound nonchalant.

"I figured you were just trying to get out of playing me," she said, smiling. Before I could reply, we were outside the nurse's office.

"Well," Jenny said. "Here you are."

I cast a glance through the wire-enforced window in the door. Inside, I could see Nurse Duckett, our school's one-woman dispenser of flu shots, throat cultures, and the occasional note of excused absence—or as we called them, "Get-out-of-jail-free cards."

Then I looked back at my escort.

Normally I would have jumped at a legitimate reason to skip out on class. But right now, it seemed more important to me to impress Jenny Kim. I mean, I didn't want her to think I was a *total* wuss.

"You know what?" I said in my manliest voice. "I don't think I need to go to the nurse's after all."

Jenny frowned at me. "But, Jack, your head—"

"—is perfectly fine," I interrupted. As proof, I rapped my knuckles against the side of my skull.

"See?" I said, even though it felt as if my brain were about to explode. "Hard as a rock."

Jenny looked doubtful. "Are you sure?" she asked.

"Sure I'm sure," I added. "No dain bramage whatsoever."

Jenny chuckled. "I suppose. If you say so . . ."

"So," I said as the second bell rang. Other students raced past us to get to homeroom before the late bell sounded. "We, um, better hurry," I said.

"Oh yeah. Right." Jenny said. "Catch you later." She smiled one last time and moved into the crowd.

It wasn't until Jenny had disappeared that it dawned on me: I still hadn't asked her out.

My first-period class was Spanish. In my experience, there is a kind of student for each foreign language:

German is for kids who are orderly and neat.

French is for girls who wear dresses and hair ribbons and have riding lessons on the weekends.

Spanish—well, Spanish is for kids who don't want to take a foreign language.

Our teacher, Mrs. Martinez, isn't from Spain. She isn't even from Mexico. She's from Boise, Idaho. She got her last name from her first husband, who was a banker or something from Argentina.

And boy, is she ever mean. If I'd been Mr. Martinez, I would have gone back to Argentina, too.

Today she was teaching us how to add numbers in Spanish. This is another example of why I don't do particularly well in school. Why would I want to add in Spanish? If I'm ever somewhere where Spanish is spoken, I intend to be having fun on a class trip. In either case I won't be doing any addition.

As my mind wandered, Mrs. Martinez's Spanish accent started sounding funny to me. It was *awful*, I suddenly realized. Truly ear-splitting. Why hadn't I ever noticed how bad her accent was before? It sounded as if she'd picked it up in a fast-food restaurant.

Wait a second. This was only my second month of Spanish. When did I become able to tell the difference between a good Spanish accent and a bad one?

My head was really pounding. I could barely concentrate.

Just listen to the way she rolls her r's, a little voice inside me said. *What's she doing, warming up for the monster truck rally?*

The sick feeling from the playground was building. And this time, it was worse. Maybe I was bleeding internally? I wondered if blood would start to come out from my eyes. Perhaps I should have gone to the nurse's after all.

I guess Mrs. Martinez must have seen me zoning out, because the next thing I knew she was right behind me. "All right, sin-your Jack," she barked. It took me a second to realize that by "sin-your" she meant "señor"—me. "Stand up and tell the class: How much is *quatro* and *dos?*"

I was in trouble. Mrs. Martinez had a reputation as the strictest teacher in the entire school. I slowly rose to my feet.

"I don't know," I said. I was definitely sick. And now I was dizzy.

"In Spanish. Say it in Spanish."

"Six?" I guessed.

"In Spanish," she shot back.

"I, uh, got hit in the head earlier," I said, feeling weaker by the moment. In another second, I was going to have to lean against the desk. "I'm not feeling too good."

Mrs. Martinez wasn't buying. She must have thought I was kidding, as usual. "In Spanish," she said. "We've spent two whole weeks going over this. What's six in Spanish?"

"I don't remember."

"Give it your best shot, mister. You're not sitting down until you do."

I looked the room over from side to side. There were a lot of staring faces. More than anything else, I just wanted to sit down. I looked back at Mrs. Martinez.

"Well?" she said, crossing her arms. "We're waiting."

I opened my mouth and took a big breath. This is what came out:

"*Yo no puedo contestarse, porque yo posiblemente he sufrido un concussión y necesito ayuda médica. A la misma vez, con respeto le pido si me puede disculpar de clase.*"

And I knew it meant:

I cannot answer you, as I may have suffered a concussion and require medical attention. In the meantime, I respectfully ask to be excused from class.

The Spanish just came to me naturally. And perfectly. Mrs. Martinez gaped at me, open-mouthed. If I could have stood where she was standing, I would be staring at me, too.

"Why, Señor Jack," she said, trying to regain her composure. "You didn't tell the class you could speak Spanish."

And it just came out, before I could stop myself:

"*No, y tu no le dijiste a la clase que aprendiste español en un Taco Bell.*"

No, and you didn't tell the class you learned Spanish in a Taco Bell.

I don't know how much time you, personally, have spent inside a principal's office. The average public school student will spend a total of eleven hours being disciplined by the time he or she graduates high school—pretty skimpy on the Jack Raynes Scale of School-Based Anguish. I'd already hit the triple digits, and I was only three months into the seventh grade.

When it came to principals' offices, I considered myself something of an expert. I'd even been sent to the superintendent's once, where they only send you if you've posed "a significant threat to the entire school."

The nicest thing about our principal's office is that we don't have one anymore. Not since Ashley Rose blew it up. Well, I guess she didn't blow it up so much as burn it down, but the way those flames shot out of the windows, you'd have thought it was packed full of TNT.

So I had to meet Principal Lower in his temporary office in the back room of the library, which they normally use for storage space. I'm glad I don't have allergies or anything, because the whole place smelled like mildew and the floor was really damp. In one corner, a bucket was catching drips from the ceiling.

If Principal Lower didn't seem too happy about his new digs, I couldn't really blame him. His "desk" was just this old beat-up table surrounded by stacks of old magazines and a rusty film projector. In the middle of the table, there was a framed photograph of the ugliest baby I have ever seen. I guess the picture had been saved from the fire; the frame looked kind of burnt around the edges.

According to the wall clock, Principal Lower chewed me out, without stopping for air, for exactly eighteen minutes, thirty-seven seconds. Respectable, but not the record for chewing me out, by a long shot. When I Krazy Glued the door to the girls' room shut, the teacher yapped at me for a full half hour.

"Do you feel sorry about what you've done?" Principal Lower asked, taking his glasses off and folding them up. That was a signal that things were about to wrap up.

"Yes, sir," I said. I didn't add what I was thinking: *I'm sorry I ever signed up for that stupid Spanish class in the first place.*

"You've embarrassed a teacher in front of her class," Principal Lower went on. "A teacher needs her class's respect to do her job. How do you expect your classmates to learn Spanish without the help of a teacher?"

"I don't know, sir," I said. Although what I was thinking was, *How do you expect Drew Molinari to learn anything without the help of a brain?*

"Well, then, in the future, try to show more respect for your elders. Do you understand, Jack? Jack?"

I'd understood just fine. But I'd also frozen. There, on the floor, emerging from a stack of old *National Geographics*, was a line of enormous black ants.

The largest ant on record weighed as much as a Quarter Pounder. These were Big Mac–size ants.

They were more like small dogs than bugs. And they were crawling right over my sneaker.

I hadn't always hated bugs so much. It started when I was seven.

Everyone knew that there was a huge collection of balls on top of our town's grammar school. Every baseball, football, handball, and Frisbee that had ever gone astray, since the building was founded in 1906, was up there.

It became my mission to make that collection my own. So one day in June, after summer vacation had started, I got up early, and using a handy maple tree as my ladder, I climbed up there.

The rumors were true. There, on the roof, was the biggest assortment of balls I'd ever seen. I started picking them up and throwing them over the side.

It wasn't until I got to the very edge of the roof that I saw this funny, gray, waffle-shaped ball.

Thinking it was some kind of baseball from the turn of the century, I picked it up and brushed it off.

Instantly, thousands of small brown bugs came pouring out of the pockmarked surface. It was a nest! I was so surprised that I lost my footing—and fell off the side of the roof. I could have broken something if I hadn't fallen into the school's enormous metal Dumpster, which was brimming with soft, rotting garbage. I heaved a sigh of relief—

And that's when I heard the roaches.

The waste bin was full of them: big, brown-red insects with hairy legs and long, twitching antennae. I screamed myself hoarse as they crawled into my shoes, up my pants legs, down the neck of my shirt.

Finally, a janitor who was wondering about all the balls on the school lawn heard my cries and came and found me. He had me out of the container in a matter of moments. But days later, I was still feeling bugs in my clothing and hair. No matter how many times I showered, I couldn't erase the memory of that morning I spent as a human roach motel.

I suddenly realized that Principal Lower was staring at me. Then I realized that he was staring at me because I was standing on my chair.

"I see we have a little pest problem," he said. "Well, Jack, if you think you've learned your lesson, I'm going to go call the janitor."

He started to get up. Was he just going to leave me there, at the mercy of the ants? Then he stopped.

"Oh, and Jack?" he said. "When you get down from there, you have a week's detention."

Chapter 5

"I just don't see how you could have learned so much Spanish in no time at all," Cleveland said, chewing contemplatively on half of a PB&J, cut along the diagonal.

The lunchroom was packed, as usual. But I noticed something funny. Everyone was looking in my direction. I mean, usually if I want people to look at me, I have to do something dumb, like ride my skateboard down a lunch table. This time they were just looking at me.

Apparently word of my newfound Spanish talent had spread.

"I don't know, either," I told Cleveland. "I guess I'm just a fast learner."

"Yeah, right," Cleveland said dryly. "And *I'm* a fast grower."

"Maybe Jack was someone else in a past life,"

Elena Vargas said. "Someone who could speak Spanish."

Elena's the only girl we let at our lunch table. Actually, I suppose she's the only girl who *wants* to sit at our lunch table.

She's pretty cool, but she's always reading books about astrology and psychic energy and the spirit world. Sometimes I think it's gone to her head. For my birthday present, she said she'd paint a picture of my aura.

"I don't believe in that past life stuff," I told her.

"Well, you can believe what you want," Elena said ominously. "But my grandmother told me that once, when she was a girl back in Mexico, a baby was born who started speaking fluent French. She thinks it was the reincarnation of Marie Antoinette."

"Oh, come on," I said. "Doesn't your grandma also talk to the TV?"

Elena frowned at me. "Well, how else do you explain what you can do?"

"I've got it," Byron Prendergast said, washing a pack of glazed donuts down with a choc-o-shake. "In a previous life, you were one of those phone guys. You know, 'Press one for English, press two for Spanish.'"

"No, *I've* got it," Nick Carlucci spoke up. "In a previous life, you were Gloria Estefan!"

Everybody at the lunch table laughed. "You know," Ben Jameson said, looking serious, "I read somewhere that the human brain is more open to learning new languages when we're very young than it ever is again. Maybe someone spoke Spanish to you when you were little and you picked it up then. Like a grandparent or a nanny."

"Hey, maybe your dad," Cleveland said, giving me a meaningful look.

Cleveland knows that my father died when I was four. I don't really know anything about him, other than that he was killed in a plane crash. I try really hard to remember him sometimes, but nothing comes back except one thing: the way he smelled when he shaved.

"Could be." I shrugged. I made a mental note to ask my mom when I got home.

Of course, I didn't get to go right home after school. I had to stay after. As you may have guessed, I was no stranger to detention hall, so I came prepared to relax. But I forgot three things.

The first thing I forgot was that on Fridays detention is held in Mr. Holland's science lab. The place smells really weird, like dead things, and it's impossible to get any sleep on those tall, hard stools.

The second thing I forgot was that Drew Molinari also had detention. Drew has detention

41

almost more often than I do, but today was different. Today he was in because of something he'd done to *me*. So I figured the way he saw it, it was my fault he was there. And that could be dangerous.

The third thing I forgot was that Ashley Rose was in the middle of a monthlong detention sentence for setting Principal Lower's office on fire. As soon as I entered the lab, there she was, giving me this really creepy look. I wanted to say something to her, but I had to keep in mind that this was Jenny's best friend.

"Hey, Raynes," Drew hissed as I passed him. "How does it feel having a girl protect you?"

"I don't know," I shot back. "How does it feel to throw like one?"

"All right, gentlemen," Mr. Holland said. He was standing in front of the classroom, unpacking cardboard crates labeled "Specimens." "Cut the conversation and take your seats."

Just get through this, I said to myself. *Just get through.*

I chose a seat in the middle of a row about one third of the way from the front. I call this area of detention hall the "Comfort Zone." It's usually far enough from the teacher so that he or she can't actually see what you're working on, but close enough so that teachers don't get overly suspicious.

Never sit in the back row. That's where they expect you to goof off.

Opening my notebook, I started to doodle. I scribbled Jenny Kim's name a few times, pretending I was working on my algebra homework. Every few minutes I'd fake like I was erasing something, or frown and bite on my pencil, or glance toward the ceiling and count on my fingers.

It's an act I've honed to perfection. I can do it in my sleep.

But today I just wasn't into it.

Something was wrong.

I was getting that funny sick feeling again, just like I'd had on the playground this morning and then again in Spanish class.

I felt dizzy. My head was beginning to throb. And there was a strange, faint buzzing noise in my ears, like the way static sounds on the radio.

Maybe that ball had hit me harder than I thought.

I raised my hand to the place where I'd been beaned by Drew's baseball, just above and behind my left ear. My fingers traced a hard, round bump. It felt as if someone had inserted half a golf ball under my scalp.

As soon as I touched it, it was as though I'd hit the volume switch on my brain. The fuzzy noise grew a zillion times louder.

I winced, shaking my head, but the strange buzzing wouldn't go away. It seemed to fill the entire lab, to come at me from every direction.

Could anyone else hear it? I looked over at

Ashley. Her nose was buried in her English note-book. If she could hear the noise, too, she gave no sign of it. Drew and Mr. Holland seemed oblivious as well.

I've got to get out of here, I thought. *I've got to get away. Got to—*

ESCAPE.

Out of the fuzziness, the single word formed. Perfectly. For one brief second, it was as if the static in my ears suddenly tuned in a station.

But just as quickly, it went back to being static.

I tried to concentrate.

Do you know those picture books, where there's just a bunch of mixed-up computer patterns, but if you focus your eyes the right way, you can see a 3-D image? This was like that, except I was doing it with my ears. Slowly, whispery words began to form out of all the fuzzy gobbledygook:

ESCAPE. MUST GET OUT. GET AWAY.

Is this what it's like when crazy people hear voices? I wondered. I had a brief mental picture of me wearing a tinfoil suit and waving a bow and arrow.

"Drew," Mr. Holland called from the front of the lab. "Could you give me a hand with these boxes?"

Drew seemed glad to ditch his homework. He slid off his stool and lumbered over to Mr. Holland's desk. "What's in these?" he asked, picking up one of the crates.

"*Arachna rogensis,*" Mr. Holland replied. "That is to say, red spiders. We're going to be doing a lab on them next week."

"Bugs, huh?" Drew said. He looked directly at me with an evil grin on his face.

Drew found out about my bug-o-phobia when I found a tick in my hair in fifth-grade gym class. It's been his secret weapon against me ever since.

"I suppose one could call them bugs," Mr. Holland said. "But they're not insects. Spiders are actually— Drew, look out!"

Carrying the largest box of all, Drew pretended to trip over the stool at the end of my row. The crate hit the ground with a loud crash, breaking open instantly.

Thousands of spiders poured across the floor.

It was like a red hairy flood running on a million spindly legs.

Straight at me.

My heart lodged in my throat. I watched in wide-eyed horror as the mass of creepy-crawlies scurried toward my legs. I couldn't move. I was frozen to the spot.

They were mere inches away when I finally found my voice.

"Get away! Get away!" I screamed. The words came out high and shrill, like fingernails on a blackboard.

And, just like that, the tide of *Arachna rogensis*

stopped dead. They seemed to recoil at the sound of my voice.

The spiders turned around and ran in the opposite direction.

"Look what you've done!" Mr. Holland yelled at Drew. "Do you know how much those cost the school?"

"Oops," Drew said brightly.

By now, the spiders had disappeared into the cracks in the walls and the floor.

Some janitor is going to be in for a surprise, I thought as my heart continued to pound in panic mode.

It wasn't until my pulse slowed down that I realized the weird buzzing noise had disappeared, too. I looked around the room, relieved—

And realized that Ashley Rose had vanished as well.

Mr. Holland was so mad at Drew that he didn't even notice that Ashley had slipped out of the lab. By three-thirty, she was ancient history. By four o'clock, I had covered an entire sheet of paper with the words "Jenny Kim," over and over again. By four-thirty, I had blacked them all out, worried it would give Drew more ammo if he saw it.

Finally, the bell rang and it was time to go.

I headed to the parking lot where my stepdad, Thad, was supposed to meet me.

Thad is pretty old, even older than my mom, but I get along with him a lot better than I do with a lot of the kids my own age. He'd been away for a week at a business thing at the state college in Madison. I couldn't wait to see him. Well, okay—I also couldn't wait to see what he'd gotten me for my birthday.

But, as usual with Thad, when I got to the parking lot, he wasn't there. I knew he'd show up eventually. It just might not be before nightfall. Thad sometimes gets so wrapped up in the things that interest him—books, mainly, and his job setting up computer systems—that he completely forgets about the rest of the world.

But that's also one of the things that's so great about Thad. He's interested in everything. He'll listen to anything you tell him, even though sometimes it seems as if there's nothing he doesn't know, and he never makes you feel stupid when you ask a question.

In fact, Thad was the one who got me started reading *The Guinness Book of Records*, which is my destiny in life, so I guess I kind of owe him one.

I shivered. It was pretty cold out and already growing dark. Thanksgiving was only two weeks off, and a fair amount of snow had fallen in the past couple weeks. Now it blew in spidery drifts across the deserted parking lot.

It looks like dancing ghosts, I thought, and then

47

scolded myself for sounding like Elena Vargas. But I was still creeped out. I was beginning to regret not taking the late bus with the other kids.

Where was Thad? Had he forgotten me?

As I waited, I nervously spun the wheels on my skateboard with my hand. The ball bearings made a light *zizzing* noise that echoed loudly against the brick building. It reminded me of the weird buzzing from detention.

What happened back there, anyway? Had Drew's fast ball simply knocked a screw loose in my brain? Or was Elena Vargas right? Was I possessed by some Spanish-speaking spirit that liked to whisper strange warnings in my brain?

I was thinking about heading back inside and watching from there—risky, because you can't see the entire parking lot, and Thad might just give up and go home—when I heard another whisper.

"Jack," it called.

This time the voice wasn't in my head. It was coming from around the corner of the school building. Not as if that made it any less scary.

"Jack, come over here a minute." It sounded urgent.

I wondered who it was. It wasn't Drew Molinari. Drew would have thrown in the word *twerp*. I moved closer.

"Who's there?" I called.

"Just come over for a second, okay?"

Then I spotted Ashley Rose's black backpack lying on the ground. So she *was* looking at me funny back in detention hall. I stepped around the corner. "Hey, Ashley," I started to say. "How did you pull off that disappearing trick?"

Then I saw who was next to her, and the words caught in my mouth.

The boy standing next to Ashley was thin, maybe ninety-five pounds, wearing a kind of dorky rugby shirt and carrying a Wolverine backpack. *Isn't he cold in just that?* I wondered.

"Hey, Ethan," I said. "What's going on?"

I used to think Ethan Rogers was a wimpy little nerd. Everyone did, until last month. First Ethan was jumped by somebody at a comic-book store. Then he was attacked by some psycho right here in the school gym.

And I thought *I* attracted trouble.

Too bad for whoever attacked him, Ethan is a seventh-grader who takes his karate *seriously*. Those guys never knew what hit them.

Afterward, Ethan became sort of popular around school—for about five minutes. Then he just went back to hanging with his dweeb friends, as if nothing happened.

The following week, Ashley Rose had her own near-death experience at the reservoir. A few days later, she torched the principal's office. She could never explain why, but everyone else could: because she's a total freak.

Ethan Rogers. Ashley Rose. The Deadly Duo of Metier, Wisconsin. It made a weird kind of sense that they were together.

But what did they want with me?

"Jack," Ethan said, stepping out of the shadows. "If you think you're going crazy, you're not."

"Uh, thanks," I said, trying to sound casual. "I don't."

I remembered the slip of paper I found in my pocket that morning. *Your life is in danger.*

"Say, I got your note."

"What note?" Ashley asked.

"We didn't send you a note," Ethan said.

"I found a note in my pocket this morning that said my life was in danger," I said.

Ashley looked at Ethan. "Someone else must know," she said.

"Know *what?*" I demanded.

"Look, Jack," Ashley said. "Since your thirteenth birthday, have you been feeling funny?"

"Noticed any weird changes?" Ethan pressed. "Strange things that are happening to you?"

"What do you mean?" I said. "Like getting hair in my armpits?"

"We're serious, Jack," Ashley persisted. "Have you been experiencing any kind of unusual sensations at all?"

50

Suddenly, I knew what they were getting at. That throbbing. The buzzing in my ears. Somehow they *knew*.

And that scared me.

How did they know? Was there something really wrong with me? Was I going to wind up a freak, like Ethan and Ashley?

"No," I lied. "I hurt my head today. That was it."

"Jack, you spoke perfect Spanish," Ashley said. "People heard you."

"So?"

"So, you don't even speak perfect English."

"Well, maybe if I had all the time in the world to sit home and study, like you and nerd boy here—"

"Jack, if you can do these things, you have to listen to us," Ashley said. "Something may try to kill you."

"You mean some*one*," I said. "*Now* who can't speak perfect English?"

"No," Ethan said. "She means some*thing*."

"We have to know," Ashley said. "And if you won't tell us, there's only one way to find out."

That was when I saw the glint of steel in her hand.

Chapter 6

"What are you going to do with that?" I asked, staring at Ashley's weapon.

It was an ordinary pin, but she held it like a dagger.

"Prick your finger," she said. "If your blood is red, you're human. If it's silver . . ."

". . . you're one of us," Ethan finished.

I laughed nervously. "'One of us'?" I asked. "What does that mean—I'm going to join the chess club?"

"One of us *nonhumans*," Ashley said quietly.

I looked from her to Ethan. They were serious. They believed what they were saying. And they were going to test their idea, one way or another.

Just then, I saw something big and white turn the corner into the school driveway. I breathed a huge sigh of relief. The cavalry had arrived.

"Hey, I'd love to give you guys a blood sample," I said, "but my ride's here. Some other time?"

Before they could answer, I slammed my skateboard against the pavement and pushed off.

"Friends of yours?" Thad asked as I climbed into his pure white Ford Galaxie 500 Supreme, surely the coolest car in existence. I slammed my door shut. I could feel Ethan's and Ashley's twin stares as I fumbled with my seat belt.

"Uh—not really."

"Do they need a ride?"

"Trust me," I said, clicking the buckle in place. "Where they're from, you need a rocket ship to get to."

Thad flashed me a huge grin as we pulled out of the parking lot. We'd soon left Ethan and Ashley far behind. I heaved a sigh of relief, then noticed that Thad was still grinning at me.

"You have to tell me," Thad said. "*What* did you say to that Spanish teacher that got her so upset?"

"I don't know," I said, trying not to smile.

"You don't *know?*" he asked. "She called the house looking for blood. Practically wanted you sent to the electric chair. She wants your mother to call her Monday morning."

"Terrific," I moaned. "Mom's gonna kill me!"

"Well, you know," Thad said, grinning that huge grin again. "We computer guys sometimes forget to pass on messages. See, we get so caught up in what we're doing that we totally lose track of our responsibilities."

"Like buying birthday presents for your adopted son?"

His face went blank. "Is it your birthday?" he asked, looking puzzled.

"Thad!" I said. "You didn't forget!"

"I didn't?" he said, looking surprised. "Oh. Then that must explain the big package sitting on your bed."

He flashed me a quick grin.

"How big?" I asked.

"Wait and see," he teased. "So, tell me," he continued. "Did you really get hit on the head? Or was it just a good way to avoid getting expelled?"

When he was my age, Thad was the master of getting out of school, so he isn't fooled by my tricks. That's one of the many things that's cool about him. I showed him my lump.

Thad whistled. "That's quite a goose egg you got there. How'd you manage that?"

"I was trying to ask out a girl," I muttered.

"Hate to say it, young blood, but if that's how she reacted, you're doing something wrong."

Tell me about it, I thought miserably.

"What did the nurse say?" he asked.

I squirmed a little in my seat. "Uh . . . nothing much," I said. *Nothing at all*, I wanted to add.

"She didn't tell you to go see a doctor?" he asked.

"No," I said, truthfully.

Thad looked over at me, concerned. "And you sure you're okay?" he asked. He held up his hands. "How many fingers, kiddo?"

"None," I replied. "Those are two thumbs."

"Aw," Thad said, retracting his thumbs and grabbing the wheel just before we went off the road. "You're too smart for me. Pretty soon you're going to get on that Internet thing, and then you kids will take over the world."

"Yeah, right," I said. "I'm lucky just to connect to AOL."

A few minutes later, we pulled into the driveway. Mom was already home.

I remembered I had something to ask her.

"Did my father ever speak Spanish?"

Mom almost dropped the bowl of mashed potatoes she was bringing to the table, where I was busy laying out the silverware.

She doesn't like to talk about my dad. She doesn't even keep a picture of him around.

"Your father?" she asked, setting the bowl down. "Why? Have people been asking you questions?"

"No—"

"Then why are you asking?" Before I knew it, Mom had taken hold of me by the shoulders. There was a look of panic in her eyes. "Are you sure? No one has been asking you about him?" She shook me a little. The forks rattled in my hand.

"Honey," Thad said. "Cut the kid some slack. He's just asking a question."

For a second, Mom just stood there, frozen, clutching tightly at my arms. Then it was as if she were waking from a trance. She blinked a couple times, looked down at her hands, then guiltily released me.

"You're right," Mom said, straightening out her hair. "I'm sorry, Jack. It's just that I . . . it's upsetting for me to think about your father. I don't believe he spoke any language besides English. Why do you ask?"

"Well, I'm suddenly good at Spanish," I said. "And I was wondering if someone spoke it to me when I was little."

"Oh, honey," Mom said, kissing me on the forehead. "Just because you excel at something doesn't mean there has to be a special reason for it. Perhaps you just have a natural talent for foreign languages."

"No, I mean I'm *really* good," I went on. "I don't think I could get to be this good on my own."

"You're way too hard on yourself, squirt," Thad said. "I always said, you can do anything you put your mind to. You're pretty bright, for a pint-size brat." He ruffled my hair.

Maybe Thad was right. Maybe I was just being

hard on myself. Maybe this was normal after all.

Nah.

Even if I hadn't spoken Spanish like a native Spaniard, or had not had that odd encounter with Ethan and Ashley, how could you explain the way Mom had just reacted? It was true that it upset her to talk about my natural father. But she hadn't *looked* upset.

She'd looked scared.

Scared for me.

I began to wonder if maybe I should be scared for me, too.

At least I wasn't as whacked out as Ashley and Ethan. Those two had truly lost their grip on Planet Earth.

That's what I kept telling myself, anyway. But a little voice inside me wasn't sure. If Ethan and Ashley were right, if I were . . . *different* . . . somehow, if my life *were* in danger—well, it would explain a lot.

I tried to question Mom further, but for the rest of our meal the conversation was all about Thad's business trip. Mom seemed to be purposely avoiding looking in my direction.

There's only one way to find out. . . .

Ashley's words echoed in my brain.

After dinner had been cleared away, I stood in the bathroom, with one of Thad's shaving razors in my hand. I was going to find out one way or another. Even if it meant bleeding for it.

I held my breath, closed my eyes, and slowly pressed the sharp metal against my fingertip.

I opened my eyes expecting to see a fountain of plasma, but all I did was leave a white line across my fingertip. No blood of any color: red, silver, or plaid. I guess I hadn't pressed hard enough.

I exhaled. I was going to have to really do it. This time, I was ready.

Again, I pushed the plastic face of the razor against my finger. Again, nothing happened.

Suddenly, I realized: There was a reason they called it a *safety* razor. I could play with it all night without cutting myself.

I opened the medicine cabinet again, looking for something to do the job. They can make glass blades with a thickness six thousand five hundred times finer than a human hair. Why didn't we have something like that lying around? Or, at least, something sharper than a Q-Tip?

My concentration was broken by a sharp knocking on the door. I slammed the medicine cabinet shut.

"What?" I yelled, annoyed.

"Hey, you've got a phone call," Thad said.

"Tell them to call back. I'm busy."

"It's a gi-*irl*," Thad sang. Honestly, there are times I really wish he would act his age.

Wait a second. A girl? As in, what Jenny Kim is?

I was out of the bathroom so fast I left skid marks.

"Hello, Jack?" said a delightfully chirpy voice on the other end of the phone line.

"Uh . . . ," I said, feeling all the air drain from my lungs. Just because Jenny was on the phone didn't make talking to her any easier than it was face-to-face.

"Is this Jack?" Jenny asked again. I could picture her face, frowning prettily, her nose crinkling—

"Yes!" I said. "Yes, this is Jack!"

"You always sound so excited when you say yes," she observed.

"Well, I'm a positive person," I said.

"It's a good quality," she said. "I'm a positive person, too. I wanted to ask how your head was."

I struggled to remember what she meant. Oh yeah. "It's fine," I said. "Thanks for asking."

"I heard what happened in Spanish class," she said. "What you did was pretty incredible."

"Oh, it's nothing, really," I said. "I think I just have a natural talent for foreign languages."

Just then I heard a sharp crackle on the line. "Hello?" said an elderly woman's voice.

"Just a minute, Grandma," Jenny said.

"You shouldn't be on the phone, Jenny," her grandma scolded. "It's too late at night! You will wake people up!"

"That's okay, Mrs. Kim," I said. "I wasn't sleeping. Jenny's just helping me with my homework."

There was a sudden click as Jenny's grandmother hung up. "I hope I didn't just get you in trouble," I said.

"You—did you actually understand what she said?" Jenny asked, incredulous.

"Sure," I shrugged. "She's kinda old, but—"

"Then you really do have a natural talent for languages," Jenny interrupted. "Jack, she was speaking Korean."

Chapter 7

I didn't know what to say to that. "Well . . . I could kind of figure out what she was saying by her tone of voice," I improvised.

"Oh," Jenny said, not sounding very convinced.

We talked for about another five minutes. I was distracted the whole time. What was going on with me? How had Ethan and Ashley known about the weird things I was going through? What did they mean—*you're one of us?*

I had to find out. I hung up with Jenny, realizing I'd just ruined yet another golden opportunity to ask her out but too worried to really care. I headed straight for the bathroom.

Thad was standing over the sink, holding his razor in one hand. I must have left it out when I ran to get the phone. "Interested in learning how to shave?" he asked, smiling at me.

"Uh . . . yeah," I lied.

"Tell you what. Tomorrow morning, meet me right here, and I'll give you lesson number one. Now, do you plan to use your own stubble, or would you like to rent some of mine?"

We talked for a little while, standing there in the bathroom. Thad had a way of making me feel safe, as though nothing in the whole world could ever be really wrong.

I didn't exactly forget about Ethan and Ashley's questions, or about Mom's weird reaction to me asking about my father, or about my sudden fluency in Spanish, and now, I guess, Korean. But suddenly they seemed like problems that could wait until morning.

So, saying good night, I retreated to my bedroom.

I slept poorly. Strange noises kept me half awake all night. My brain felt as if it had swollen up inside my skull and was throbbing against the sides. Facts from *The Guinness Book* came to me during the night, all of them about foreign languages:

- Ziad Fazah, of Brazil, can speak 58 languages, more than any other person in history.
- More people speak Chinese than anything else.
- The Ample language, spoken in Papua New Guinea, has over 69,000 finite verb forms and 860 infinitive verb forms. (I have no idea what this last fact means. I just memorized it.)

Finally, I drifted off to sleep.

What seemed like ten minutes passed before I awoke again, this time because my bed was violently shaking. Dreading what I'd find, I opened my eyes.

What I saw in front of me was more grotesque, more horrible than anything out of a nightmare. It was all I could do not to scream.

"Cleveland," I said, instead, trying to avert my eyes from his big, stupid face. "Why are you shaking my bed?" Cleveland was no beauty pageant winner by day, but this early in the morning he was ugly enough to cut glass.

"Because," he said simply, "you're sleeping. And you have to get up."

"Why do I have to get up?" I whined.

"You'll understand when we get there," he shot back. "Get up. Throw some clothes on."

"Shouldn't I shower?" I asked.

"It's Saturday," he pointed out.

"Oh," I replied. "Good point."

Fifteen minutes later, we were on our skateboards heading into the center of town.

"Cleveland," I said as we neared the mall. "You said you were going to tell me why you woke me up." I was still dead tired. If it were possible, I was even more tired that morning than I was the night before.

"I am," he said. "I am. All in good time."

We rounded the corner and came to the mall's back parking lot. It was packed. Loaded with cars and swarming with people. What were they doing here so early?

"Cleveland, what time is it?" I asked.

"Noon," he answered.

I guess I'd slept later than I thought. "And what are all these people doing here?" I asked. Judging from the number of people coming in and out of the big building, you'd have thought there were only a few shopping days left until Christmas. Had I slept straight through Thanksgiving?

"They're here for that," he said proudly, pointing to an enormous Winnebago parked by the mall entrance. It was one of those massive campers, like a small house with a speedometer. Only this one was painted green and pink and looked sort of like a giant watermelon.

The minute I saw it, I knew what it was.

"The Weirdmobile?" I asked, groaning.

"Yes, it's the Weirdmobile," Cleveland said in his fake show-announcer voice. "And standing behind it is Gil Shepherd, the host of *Too Weird!* coming to you today straight from—are you ready for this?"

"Don't tell me."

"Metier, Wisconsin!" he shouted.

"The only town in America where just living there qualifies you as weird," I said.

Too Weird! is one of Cleveland's favorite TV shows. The host, this obnoxious Australian guy named Gil Shepherd, gets people to come onstage and make complete idiots of themselves while everyone laughs.

And when I say they do stupid stuff, I don't just mean moderately stupid stuff. I mean truly, deeply, earth-shatteringly stupid stuff, like eating chili dogs through their nose, or knitting scarves from their own hair, or juggling baked hams with their feet.

"I'm going to belch out *The Star Spangled Banner!*" Cleveland said, clearly thinking this was the smartest idea he'd ever heard.

"*That's* what you woke me up for?" I demanded. "So I could watch you make a fool out of yourself?"

"Nope," Cleveland said. "You'll know why you're here in a few minutes." He gave me his best Indiana Jones smile. "Trust me."

I rubbed my aching eyes and we shouldered our way into the crowd. I noticed a lot of them were wearing costumes. We passed a woman dressed like a banana, and a group of shirtless guys with the letters W-E-I-R-D spelled out in red greasepaint on their naked stomachs.

Finally, we arrived around the front of the Weirdmobile.

From this side you could see how the crazy,

polka-dotted vehicle actually converted into its own mini TV studio. It was really pretty cool. A giant antenna telescoped up from its roof, and the whole rear section unfolded to reveal a dazzling stage set.

On stage, a toothpick-skinny guy wearing extralarge sunglasses, a zipper tie, and a red fez cleared his throat into a microphone. It was Gil Shepherd, looking just like he did on TV, which is to say like a Chihuahua that's been through a taffy puller. The crowd went crazy.

"We're just in time!" Cleveland yelled at me over the hubbub.

"Oh, goody," I said, rolling my eyes.

Gil was just getting into his routine. "G'day, mates, and welcome to another exciting episode of *Too Weird!* brought to you today by the wild and wacky people of . . . Metier, Wisconsin!" When he said, "Metier, Wisconsin," the whole crowd went insane.

Who does this guy think he is, I thought. *Crocodile Dundee?*

"We've got a lot of prizes today," Gil said in his heavy Australian accent, "including a lifetime supply of dental floss, a psychic reading from Madame Mysteria, and of course . . . the half-ton bar of chocolate!"

I winced. What do you even *do* with a half-ton bar of chocolate once you've won it? Stand on it to get things off high shelves?

Gil moved center stage. "So without further ado—or, should I say, *odd*-do—Metier, Wisconsin . . . *Whoooo's weeeeeird?*" he howled.

The crowd went ape. People were climbing over each other to get closer to the stage. It was a sea of hands, each person trying to be seen and selected by the fabulous Gil. Some people even had homemade signs and banners reading "I'm Weird!" or "Pick Me, Gil!"

"*Whoooo's weeeeird?*" Gil chanted, twirling around like a top. "*Whoooo's weeeeird? Whoooo's weeeeird? Whoooo's weeeeird?*"

"*This,*" Cleveland said, "is why you're here."

"You mean, you want me to get his attention for you? Because I'm taller than you and he might see my hand better than yours? You woke me up for that?"

"Yup," Cleveland said simply.

You've got to say this for Cleveland: He thinks ahead.

"Okay," I said. "But this is the last time."

I had done this for Cleveland at every baseball tournament, autograph signing, and video game convention we'd been to since we were ten. By now, I considered myself something of a professional attention-getter.

There's a knack to being called on in a large crowd. You have to stand somewhere clearly visible to the person doing the choosing. You have to really *want* to be called on.

And—this is the key—you have to work in short bursts at nuclear-grade volume. I'm talking loud enough to crack things.

I got into position. Then I let fly: "Over Here!" I hollered, jumping up and down. "Right! Over! Here!" I was loud enough that the couple standing next to me, dressed in matching rubber scuba gear, turned and stared at me in astonishment.

Immediately, Gil stopped spinning and pointed straight at me.

Wow, that was fast, I thought. I'd like to think it was a matter of skill, but given the events of my recent past, it may just have been that I registered really high on the weird radar. Then, to my alarm, I found myself being pushed forward by a sea of hands.

"Hey! Not me, him!" I yelled desperately, pointing back toward Cleveland. "Him! Him!"

Before I could stop them, the audience had pushed me right up on stage. There I was, looking directly over hundreds of my fellow Metierites and into the big single lens of a TV camera. I tried to protest, but it was too late.

I was on.

Chapter 8

I won't lie to you: I was a little nervous. In fact, I thought I was going to heave right onto Gil Shepherd's orange-and-purple plaid sports coat. Of course, that jacket already looked as if someone *had* upchucked on it.

"And what's your name, my eager young man?" Gil bellowed, thrusting his mike into my face.

"J-Jack," I stammered. I pointed into the crowd to where a big brown fedora was frantically bobbing up and down. "I'm, uh, actually here for, um, Cleveland—"

Gil snatched the mike away. "Let's hear it for Jack, who's come all the way from Cleveland, Ohio!"

The crowd applauded and whistled. I grinned at them like a moron and began to wish that I'd taken that shower.

Yikes. This isn't going the way I planned.

"So, Jack," Gil said, clamping his hand down on my shoulder. "What's your special talent?"

My mind went blank. I looked over the audience. Hundreds and hundreds of people, all waiting to hear what I had to say. My eyes scanned the sea of staring faces.

Gil gave my shoulder a sharp squeeze.

"Uh! I can . . . um . . . speak Spanish," I said, feebly.

Gil frowned. "Well, there's nothing too weird about that, Metier, is there?" He laughed. *Everybody* laughed.

"Get off the stage!" someone yelled. Other people started booing.

"Go back to Cleveland!" shouted the guy with the letter *R* on his belly.

Great, I thought. *It's Saturday, I barely slept, and my entire hometown is laughing at me.* My ears started burning and my head started to throb. Dimly, I wondered if I'd just broken the record for the most humiliated man alive.

I made a mental note to kill Cleveland on sight.

"I speak the Greek!" a big, dark-haired man in a black pea coat shouted at the stage. His accent was so thick, you could have sliced it and made sandwiches. "I am my entire life the Greek speaking! Give to me the prize!"

Suddenly my head felt as if it were being crushed

72

in a vise. I opened my mouth to say "ouch." Instead, this came out:

"*Borí na milás Elliniká, allá sígoura then borís na milísis Angliká.*"

I was startled to hear the strange words reverberate against the walls of the mall, a football field's distance away. I'd forgotten I was speaking into a mike.

The crowd fell silent. The man in the pea coat looked as if he were about to explode.

"*What* did you say?" Gil Shepherd asked, suddenly quiet.

"I told him, 'Maybe you can speak Greek, but you sure can't speak English,'" I said, too stunned to cover it up.

The crowd laughed. I suppose they liked me after all!

"But," Gil said, "unless I miss my guess, you said it the first time in Greek!"

I realized he was right. I *had* just spoken in Greek, without even knowing it. Fluently.

What was going on?

"How about Dutch?" Gil asked with a gleam in his eye. "Can you insult that fellow in Dutch?"

As soon as Gil said "Dutch," my head throbbed painfully.

"*In plaats van je duim in een dijk te steken, probeer je hoofd erin te steken.*" I shot back.

"And what was that in English?" Gil asked.

"'Instead of sticking your thumb in a dike,'" I translated, "'try your whole head.'"

The crowd roared. "Can you insult him in Japanese?" Gil asked.

Again, my head pounded. Worse this time.

"Amari futto te zubon wa sumo-tori no saizu," I said. "You're so fat, your pant size is 'sumo.'"

My head was growing more and more painful by the moment. Little pinpricks of light started dancing around the edges of my vision—

But the audience loved my act! They were howling with laughter. They even started calling out requests.

"Chinese!"

Throb!

"In China, they eat things smarter than you."

"Arabic!"

Throb!

"If Aladdin had another wish, he would have wished that you start using deodorant."

"Hindu!"

Throb!

"You're so dumb, you thought a snake charmer was something you wear on a friendship bracelet."

The throbbing in my head was unbearable. I could feel my legs going numb. Everything was spinning.

"Australian!"

"You're so ugly . . . ," I said, and paused.

74

"Well?" Gil asked in his thick Australian accent. "G'wan, mate." His voice sounded far, far away.

"You're so ugly," I repeated, "that once . . . someone mistook you for . . . Gil . . . Shepherd."

I don't know what the audience reaction was to that, because suddenly I fell forward. And everything went black.

Chapter 9

When I woke up, I was in a strange bed. *At least I'm in a bed*, I thought, *and Cleveland isn't here to bug me.*

When I opened my eyes, I saw Mom and Thad standing over me. They looked very blurry. And very worried. I waited for them to say something, but the next thing I heard was a woman's voice—unfamiliar, yet somehow comforting.

"You're in the hospital, Jack."

A blinding light pierced my vision. I would have struggled if I wasn't so tired. As it was, I just lay back and waited as the light shone first in one eye, then the other.

"You passed out," the voice continued, gently. "But everything's going to be fine now."

When they say that in sci-fi books, it means *nothing's* going to be okay. I bit my lip and waited for the face behind the light to turn out to be a monster, or a gruesome reptile, or an eight-foot bug.

Instead, when the light clicked off, I found myself staring into the clear blue eyes of a gray-haired woman in a white coat. She had a stethoscope around her neck.

I guess sometimes you can't go by the books.

"I'm Doctor Strickrichter," the woman said. "You're a very lucky boy. I hear you got hit on the head yesterday in school?"

I nodded.

"And why didn't you go to the nurse's office?" my mother demanded. I winced, too embarrassed to tell her the real reason.

"The important thing is that he's seeing a doctor now," Dr. Strickrichter said, coming to my rescue. "Jack, you've suffered a concussion. If you had gone much longer before receiving medical attention, you could have had fluids accumulate in your brain and suffered some real damage."

"Is he going to be okay?" Thad asked, genuinely worried.

"He's totally fine," the doctor said. "Or he looks that way. We're going to run some tests to be absolutely sure. A CAT scan and some other things."

"Check to see if it's his adult brain growing in," Thad said. "His baby brain was ready to fall out, anyway."

"Quit it," I said. "Can't you see that I'm a dying boy?"

"You are *not* dying," Mom said, taking things much too seriously as usual.

"Come on," the doctor said, wheeling my cot out of the room. "Let's get you in a nice, hot CAT scan."

We passed through a series of double doors and under a bronze plaque that said "Neurology" in big black letters. That troubled me. I have a motto that has served me well over the years: Never get into a medical condition you can't spell.

"There you go," said the doctor, wheeling me to a stop. "I'll be back in about a half hour and then we can run those tests. In the meantime, you can watch TV, or read a magazine, or just relax." She smiled at me, and left.

There was a kid in the bed next to me playing one of those ultra-new, not-available-until-Christmas Gameboys.

Wish I had one, I thought.

I grabbed the remote off the counter and flipped through the stations on the wall-mounted television. Suddenly, the screen showed the parking lot of the Metier Mall. It was the closing credits of *Too Weird!*

"Hey, I was on that show!" I exclaimed. My roommate didn't even look over.

"So, until next time, America," Gil Shepherd

drawled on the television. *"Whooooooooo's weee—"*

I clicked off the TV, cutting him off in mid-howl.

Four P.M. on a Saturday: It was the TV deadlands. Nothing would be on except golf and boat racing until seven-thirty at the earliest.

I tried to close my eyes, to relax, but it was no good. I wasn't going to get to sleep.

I made a mental note to kill Cleveland *twice*.

Finally, I flipped over and looked at the kid playing the Gameboy.

He looked to be a year or two younger than me, probably a sixth-grader. He had curly, kinky blond hair and bright green eyes. I wondered where he was from.

"Wow," I said. "Is that really *Twisted Metal Three?*"

Normally, I wouldn't have been caught dead talking to a lowly sixth-grader, but this was a special circumstance. We were bunk buddies. Plus, if I was nice to him, I figured I might get a few games out of it.

He didn't answer.

"My name is Jack," I said. "Jack Raynes."

He didn't answer.

I knew what was going on. He was one of those kids whose parents get them everything in advance, and therefore think they're cooler than anyone else in the world. Oh yes: I knew his type.

80

"If you don't want to talk, fine," I said. "Be a snob. See if I care."

He didn't answer.

Just then a student nurse walked in, holding a clipboard. "Who wants a snack?" she said brightly. She looked at the name on my chart. "Jack," she said. "Would you like a snack? We have a special this afternoon: chocolate chip cookies."

"Sure," I said.

"How many would you like?"

"What number is all of them?" I asked.

She giggled and made a note on her clipboard. Then she walked over to Snob Boy. She started to make funny signs in the air with her hands. It looked like sign language.

It *was* sign language. Suddenly, I realized: Snob Boy wasn't Snob Boy at all. Snob Boy was Deaf Boy. He hadn't heard a word I said!

Sometimes I'm so smart, I slay myself.

But then something weird happened.

As the student nurse was taking his order, I became fascinated with the way her hands moved. What at first seemed like a series of random gestures slowly fell into a pattern.

It's as if she's writing her questions in the air, I thought. All at once, I felt words forming in the back of my brain.

To my amazement, when Deaf Boy signed back, I understood him perfectly. He asked for three cookies and some peanut butter to spread between them—an excellent combination, if I do say so myself.

The student nurse waved good-bye, then headed out of the room. When I turned back to my roommate, I saw that he was looking in my direction.

Before I knew what I was doing, my hands leapt into the air. "Hi," I signed. "My name's Jack. Is that really *Twisted Metal Three?*"

"Yes," he signed back. "You sign well. Where did you learn?"

"I just kind of . . . picked it up," I signed. "I didn't even know they had *Twisted Metal Three*. Where did you get it?"

"It's not available in America yet," he signed back. "But my parents got it for me from Japan. My name is Raymond. Would you like to play a game or two?"

"Would I?" I asked.

Just then, Doctor Strickrichter poked her head in the room. "Jack Raynes," she said. "Time to stick you in a big metal tube."

Some days, you just can't win.

She wasn't kidding about sticking me in a big metal tube. That was the CAT scan. What she failed to mention were the ear and nose probes, the urine samples, and the butt-exposing medical gown. Finally, after an evening of humiliations that

82

made *Too Weird!* seem mild, I was wheeled into the observation ward for some rest.

The lights were already out when I arrived—a good thing, since I was still in the gown. But it was also pretty spooky. By now it was late at night. I lay in the dark, listening as footsteps echoed down the long hospital corridor: my nurse, heading back to her station.

I felt all alone. Despite the call button by my bed, I wasn't sure I could get hold of anyone if there was an emergency. What if they missed something and my head started to swell up? What if my brain exploded before help arrived?

After a few moments, my eyes adjusted to the darkness. I peered through the gloom, trying to see what was around me.

And then I wished I hadn't.

Because I *wasn't* alone.

In the bunk next to me was what looked like a member of the living dead. Bandages extended from his head to his feet. I realized he was a burn victim, not a mummy, but my imagination was running wild. I've always been a little scared of the dark, and when you add to that a creepy hospital ward—well, at that point, Tweety Bird would have freaked me out.

"Please, Mr. Burn Victim," I said softly. "Don't get up and kill me."

I waited. And waited. After an hour had passed

without him getting up and killing me in any way, I started to feel drowsy.

And then, all of a sudden, I was asleep.

I woke up again in the middle of the night. I felt strangely comforted, as if I were in the middle of a big hug. I also felt weighted down. When had they put so many blankets on me? Did I ask for them?

In fact, I was feeling a little *too* warm. I was feeling downright hot. Almost smothered. And why was the bed moving?

I tried to sit up.

I couldn't.

I tried to say something, but there was a thick wad of cotton in my mouth. I tried to lift my arms, but they were held fast by tight canvas straps.

I was wrapped in bandages, I realized, from head to foot. And my cot was really starting to move. Had they mistaken me for the burn victim? I looked over at the burn victim's cot, as it got smaller in the distance. It was covered with gauze wrappings—as if someone had just unwrapped himself.

A chilling thought rushed into my brain. Was it the burn victim pushing me? What diabolical plans did he have for me? Did he want to trade his grisly, charred hide for my own fresh, young skin?

Was this the end?

We stopped at a nurse's station. "I'm just transport-ing this patient for tests," Dr. Strickrichter's calm voice said from behind me.

So *she* was the one pushing me after all. Well, that was a relief. But why was I bound and gagged?

"Hey, what's going on here?" I tried yelling, but it came out all muffled and funny through the cotton wad.

"He sounds bad," the nurse commented.

"Mmm-hmm," Doctor Strickrichter said.

It's no use knowing a thousand languages when you can't even open your mouth to speak, I thought.

The doctor wheeled me into an elevator. *Maybe this is just a mistake*, I thought. I twisted my head around to look up at the doctor, thinking I might be able to communicate something through my eyes.

But when I saw her face, my heart stopped.

Where her eyes were supposed to be were two big black disks that seemed to suck in the light.

This wasn't Doctor Strickrichter.

This was an alien.

The elevator doors shut silently like a tomb.

Chapter 10

I struggled against the restraints, but it was no good. The canvas straps held me tightly, biting into my bare wrists. The creature that was kidnapping me smiled evilly, mocking my struggles as the elevator descended.

Ding.

Two floors below, the doors opened to let in two more passengers. *Good*, I thought. *When they see her eyes, they'll go for help.*

Or maybe they'll just fight it out with the creature right here in the elevator, which would be twice as cool. But when I looked at its eyes, my hopes were dashed: They were back to normal.

I screamed for help, gagging on the cotton cloth, but my screams fell on deaf ears.

Literally, I suddenly realized. The other occupants of the elevator were Raymond and a muscular intern who was pushing his cot. I tried to get their attention. Unfortunately, though our cots were practically touching, Ray wasn't looking at me. As for the intern, he was wearing a loud Walkman.

I looked at the deaf boy's hand, resting by his side, only half a foot from where I lay helpless. *I'm six inches from rescue*, I thought. *And five minutes from certain death.*

If I could just grab his hand. . . .

I stretched my fingers toward his own, ignoring the pain as the strap's metal buckle dug into my flesh.

Ding.

The doors opened again. The creature started to wheel me out. This was it.

With a last, desperate lunge, I snagged the cuff of Raymond's sleeve and tugged for all I was worth. He looked over, startled. Then a look of recognition crossed his face.

"Hey, Jack," he signed. "What happened to you?"

Suddenly, I realized I couldn't move my arms! I had no way to sign to him what was going on! All I could do was use my one free hand to spell out the situation, letter by letter.

"H-E-L-P," I signed. "N-O-T M-Y D-O-C-T-O-R. B-E-I-N-G K-I-D-N-A—"

With a jolt, the creature rolled me into the hallway. The doors glided shut behind me. I was too slow. I hadn't finished the message.

My heart sank. It was all over now.

The exit sign loomed ahead, glowing red in the dim corridor. I knew that when we went through it, I was as good as dead.

Suddenly, I heard a wrenching noise behind me. It was the elevator doors being forced open! The big intern stepped out. "Hey, Doc!" he shouted. "Where are you taking that patient?"

All I could do was lie back and listen to the sounds of the intern chasing the creature down the hall. I wished I could watch, or better yet, follow them.

I felt small, swift hands unfastening my straps. I was finally able to sit up. Raymond helped me loosen my bandages enough to wriggle out of them. I brought my fingertips to my mouth, then extended both hands toward him, palm-up: "Thank you."

"Nothing to it," Raymond signed back. "Why didn't you speak up sooner?"

After a few moments, the muscular intern came back, panting. "She just vanished," he said. "But don't worry. I've alerted hospital security. They're surrounding the building. Are you okay?"

I didn't answer. Raymond looked at me. "Jack, you're not worried about that woman, are you?" he signed to me.

"No," I signed back. And I wasn't.

I was looking at my wrists. The straps had cut into my skin. I was bleeding.

And the blood was silver.

I wasn't worried.

I was scared out of my mind.

If you ever discover that you're some kind of mutant creature with bizarre secret abilities and a body that only *looks* human, my best advice is: Get some sleep the night before. Because I guarantee you won't sleep that night. Or at least, I didn't.

Hospital security found nothing. Whoever tried to kidnap me just disappeared into the night. They contacted the police, but unfortunately there wasn't much Raymond or the intern could tell them.

As for my own version of the story, I figured I'd better keep it to myself. If I started telling people about a burn victim that morphed into an eyeless version of Doctor Strickrichter in the middle of the night, they might put me in the neurology wing for good.

Several hours past dawn, the real Doctor Strickrichter came to see me. She held a fat manila folder in her hand. She smiled at me pleasantly. "I hear you had quite a wild night," she said.

"I guess," I said. "I spent most of it lying down."

"Well, I got your test results back. And I have bad news for you."

My heart skipped a beat. Did they know? Had they found out? Was I going to become a living lab rat? I had visions of brain surgery, scalpels, beady-eyed scientists studying my head under huge microscopes—

"The news is," she continued, "you have to go home. You're completely normal. No more lying in bed all day. Tomorrow it's back to school."

"I'm *normal?*" I said, realizing I was talking much louder than anyone would if they weren't, say, standing right next to a jet engine during takeoff.

"That's right. You had some pretty high activity in the speech center of your brain, but—are you taking a foreign language in school?"

"Yes," I admitted.

"Well, that could explain it," she said. "Now, I want you to go home and relax. No sports, no skateboarding, and no getting knocked unconscious for at least a week."

"But—" I started.

"No 'buts,' Mister. I mean it. You're on getting-knocked-unconscious suspension for all of next week. Now, go get dressed."

Mom fussed over me the entire ride home, smoothing down my hair, kissing the lump on my head, being sickeningly momlike. I know she was just worried for me, but there are times I wish Thad was my only close relative.

"Does it hurt, honey?" she asked for the fourth time that car ride.

"No, Mom. It still doesn't hurt," I said.

We made the familiar turn onto the little road I grew up on. It was as if I were seeing everything for the first time. Mrs. Tragos's salmon-pink house on the corner, the row of evenly spaced cedars on the Hilgards' lawn that we used to hide behind, the funny bump halfway down the street—perfect for catching air, if you're ready for it, and perfect for a quick trip to the emergency room if you're not—it felt as if I were remembering someone else's childhood. Not mine.

The only thing that gave me any comfort was when we actually pulled into my own driveway. There was the Indian corn I'd hung on the front door. There was the dent in the drainpipe from when I tried parking Thad's car. I heard the crunch of gravel underneath the station wagon's tires as we ground to a stop. I'd know that sound anywhere.

I might not be human, but I was home.

For a moment, I could almost believe that the events of the previous night hadn't happened. For a moment, I could fool myself into believing it was all in my head. And then I saw the van.

Chapter 11

The van was jet black, a weird obsidian that seemed to suck in all the light. It was parked on the grass behind the garage. There were shadowy figures inside it.

"Now who do you suppose that is?" Mom asked. Then she saw my face. "What's wrong?" she asked.

I couldn't answer. All I could do was watch as two big men lumbered out of the van and headed toward the car.

"Is this the Raynes's residence?" one of them asked.

"Say 'no,'" I whispered.

Mom smiled at the men. "Don't mind him. He's just gotten out of the hospital," she explained. "Yes, this is the Raynes's residence. Can I help you?"

"Yeah," he said. "We're here with the chocolate."

Even I was thrown by that.

"Excuse me?" Mom asked. "What chocolate?"

"I'm Moe," he said. "With *Too Weird!* Productions.

Your son here won the grand prize. It's a half-ton bar of chocolate."

I could scarcely believe my ears. I made a mental note to find someone gullible enough to buy a thousand-pound bar of chocolate. Byron Prendergast's birthday was coming up—he'd probably have some ready cash. He certainly had the appetite.

"They said they never seen anybody so weird," the delivery man continued. "They wrote you this note." He handed an envelope to my mother. She opened it, withdrawing a piece of stationery bearing the *Too Weird!* logo. We read its contents together.

```
Dear Jack,
   We have seen many strange and
incredible   performances   over
the  years,  but  yours  was  the
strangest. Had we not witnessed
your   bizarre   combination   of
speaking foreign languages and
blacking out, we would not have
thought  it  was  possible.  You
will occupy a place of honor in
the Weird! files. Please accept
this   thousand-pound   bar   of
chocolate  as  a  token  of  our
esteem—and if you're going to
```

speak Australian in the future,
be sure to stop before you need
medical attention.

                    Sincerely,
                    Gil Shepherd
                    and the entire Staff
                        of *Too Weird!*

P.S. Look for yourself in our
season-end "World of Weird"
spectacular!

"Isn't that nice?" Mom said when we had finished
reading.

"Which?" I asked. "The part where they said I
was the strangest thing they'd ever seen, or the part
where they asked me not to hurt myself?"

By this time, the delivery men were wheeling out
an enormous crate, as big as a refrigerator, on a
dolly. My eyes bugged out. That was all chocolate?
My problem wasn't going to be selling it—it was
going to be lugging it around!

"Where do you want it?" Moe asked.

That night, we had to keep Thad's Galaxie outside, because the block of chocolate took up an

entire half of the garage. Normally, he would never have let his prized possession stay outdoors overnight, even when it was mild—and the weather bureau had just issued a winter storm warning. But he didn't say anything about it. He just went outside to throw a tarp over the big automobile.

I watched him from the family room window, rolling his birthday present to me—a genuine Foundation longboard autographed by Jon West—back and forth across the carpet. Despite Doctor Strickrichter's "no skateboarding" orders, I couldn't wait to take it out for a spin.

Outside, Thad tightened the canvas straps that would hold the sheet down in high winds. I felt the chafed skin on my wrists and thought, *I know how that car feels.*

He and Mom were being ultracareful around me. I guess they were just afraid to get me upset, with my head condition and all. They made no mention of the abduction attempt. Instead, we talked about the weather: Would it snow, or would it just rain?

"New rule, bub," Thad said. "Ever since they got those new tires for the school bus, the county says you need eight full inches of snow to close the schools."

"Yeah?" I asked, not really listening. I was still thinking about the situation I was in. I needed some answers. Fast.

"Of course," Mom said much too quickly,

"you can stay home from school tomorrow, if you want to."

"That's okay," I said. "I think I can manage."

Besides, I added to myself, *there are a couple friends I want to see.*

The minute Mom and Thad left me alone, I was on the phone to Ethan's house. To my surprise and dismay, Ashley picked up.

"Rogers residence," she said.

"I need to talk to Ethan," I said. "It's Jack."

There was a moment of silence.

"I thought you didn't want our help," she said coldly.

"I changed my mind," I said. "Can I just talk to Ethan, please?"

After a minute, I heard Ethan's voice on the other end of the line. "Jack," he said. "We heard about the hospital. What happened?"

I filled him in on the details. He didn't seem surprised.

"Did you see its eyes?" he asked.

"I saw where its eyes were supposed to be," I said.

"Did you tell anyone what really happened?" he asked.

"Are you kidding?" I said. "No one would believe me. Even I don't believe me. I keep hoping I'm going to wake up."

"You're awake," he assured me. "And you need to meet with us right away."

*   *   *

Mom didn't like the idea.

"On a Sunday night?" she demanded.

"I have a lot of homework," came my reasonable reply.

"You've been through a very serious ordeal," Mom said. "I'm sure your teachers will give you an extra day."

"Please, Mom?" I said. "I'll only be gone an hour."

Mom stared at me, biting her lip. "Well, I must say, it is a pleasant surprise to see you want to do your homework for once. But I don't like the idea of you walking all alone in the dark, with the ice. . . ."

"The library is only two blocks away," I reassured her. "And it's not that icy." Geez. I had just been kidnapped by a bug-eyed monster from outer space, and here my mother was, worried that I'd slip on the sidewalk.

In the end, the image of "Jack Raynes, Honor Student," triumphed over motherly concern.

"Maybe you should have been knocked in the head a long time ago," she joked as I bundled into my coat. I pecked her on the cheek, snatched up my new skateboard, and was out the door before she could change her mind.

When I got to the library, they were already there, waiting by the reference section.

"How's your head?" Ethan asked.

"Fine," I said.

"Too bad," Ashley said.

"Come on, Ash," Ethan started.

"I've got to tell him," she said.

"Tell me what?" I asked.

"Look, Jack," she said. "This is a serious situation. Our lives are in danger. You've never been anything but the class clown. Why should we believe we can depend on you? How do we know that at the last second you won't pull a Han Solo?"

"What Ashley's trying to say is," Ethan said delicately, "we're going to have to trust one another with our lives. If you want our help, you have to be serious. We need your total commitment."

"Believe me," I said. "After last night, I *am* serious." I realized that, for once in my life, I *wasn't* joking around. I meant what I said. "I'm scared, guys. I need your help. If you trust me, I won't let you down."

"I believe you," Ethan said.

Ashley still looked suspicious, but finally she said grudgingly, "All right."

We shook on it, a three-way shake.

"Okay," I said eagerly. "Where do we start?"

"It's like any puzzle," Ethan said. "Start with the edges."

_____ Chapter 12

The "edges," by Ethan's way of thinking, were our similarities, the things we had in common. It wasn't hard to find them. Apart from last names that started with an *R*, silver blood, and the fact that our powers manifested on our thirteenth birthdays, we all had unusual family lives.

Ethan was adopted after his birth parents' boat was found floating in the middle of Lake Constance, twenty miles outside Metier—without them in it. Ashley's mother had disappeared when Ashley was still little. My father had died in a plane crash. It seemed like a pretty big coincidence.

"When did your mom disappear?" I asked Ashley.

"When I was four," she said. "She went out to get some groceries and then . . . I remember waiting all night for her to come back. But she never did."

She acted as though it didn't bother her. She'd probably said those same words so many times that they didn't mean anything to her anymore. But I knew that somewhere deep inside her was a big hole that would never be filled.

I knew because I had the same hole inside me. I pictured little Ashley Rose, four years old, sitting up all night, waiting to see her mother's headlights come up the driveway. Some part of her was still waiting.

Part of me was still waiting, too. Part of me was still hoping that the whole world was wrong, that my father wasn't dead after all, that it had all been a big mistake. That one day he would walk through the front door and laugh as he explained where he'd been for the last nine years.

"They thought maybe she'd been hit by a drunk driver—it was July Fourth and there were a lot of parties going on," Ashley continued. "But the next day they found her car, parked in front of the shopping mall. She wasn't in it."

Something clicked. "Wait a minute. They found her car on July fifth?" I asked.

"Yes," Ashley said. "Why?"

"My father's plane went down in an electrical storm on July fifth. It happened just after midnight."

"That's too much of a coincidence," Ashley said. "Ethan, what do you think?"

"Well, if *that's* not too much," Ethan said, "this is:

My parents' boat was found on the morning of the fifth."

We all sat there for a moment, a little stunned. I was trying to figure out what it all meant. Finally, I said, "Does this mean our parents might still be alive?" My voice sounded very small.

"Maybe," Ethan said.

"I think it's stupid to get our hopes up," Ashley said. "As far as I'm concerned, my mother is dead. We've got to concentrate on saving *our* lives."

"You're right," Ethan said. "Let's get to work."

We spent the next hour pouring over old newspapers, magazines, and microfiches. Ethan was sure that if we looked hard enough, we'd find a clue of some kind. Unfortunately, we had no idea what we were looking for.

"So," I said as I flipped through a yellowed copy of the *Metier Post*, "what powers do you guys have, exactly?"

"When I'm in danger," Ethan said, "my reflexes, my agility, speed, and strength all go off the charts. It's like I'm some kind of fighting machine. I think I was *engineered* to be a perfect warrior. I know martial arts, can handle any weapon, and even have heat-sensing vision, so I can see in the dark." He paused to take a breath. "Oh yeah—I nearly forgot: I also have a venomous bite, like a snake. That's how I defeated the assassin that was sent for me."

103

Before I could respond, Ashley started to speak.

"I'm subaquatic," she said. "I can stay underwater for hours on end, dive like Greg Louganis, and swim at high speeds. I have telephoto vision and supersensitive hearing. I can withstand freezing temperatures, and if I'm injured, I can heal myself—you know, regenerate new tissue. If I'm in *real* trouble, I can even split completely in half, like a planarian worm. Each half becomes a perfect replica of myself."

"Wow," I said. I didn't know what else *to* say.

"And what do you know about *your* powers?" Ethan asked.

"Yeah. What can *you* do?" Ashley said.

They both stared at me expectantly.

"I can . . . er . . . speak foreign languages," I said.

"Right," Ashley said. "We know that. What else?"

"Nothing else," I said, feeling downright shortchanged. "That's it."

"That's *it?*" Ashley asked, incredulous. "So what are you supposed to do if we get attacked by an assassin—insult him in Swahili?"

"Hey!" I said. "I didn't *pick* my powers, okay? Not everyone gets to be engineered to be a perfect warrior."

"Jack's powers can be just as significant as ours, in the right situation," Ethan said. He nodded at me. "There's an X-Man who has language abilities like yours. Without his help, they never would have stood a chance against Megator."

"Oh, brother," Ashley said, clearly unimpressed.

"Hey," I said. "Look at this."

It was just a little article, no more than two inches long, pushed way to the back of the *Post*. Clearly, the editors didn't think much of it.

"'Local man sees flying saucers over Metier Reservoir,'" Ethan read. "'A Metier resident, returning from a Fourth of July picnic, claims to have seen alien spacecraft hovering over the town reservoir. Police have been notified, but are skeptical of the man's claims.'"

"So?" Ashley said. "People see strange things over the reservoir all the time. He probably ate something funny at the picnic."

"Look at the picture," I said.

The fuzzy black-and-white square showed a clean-shaven man about Thad's age, wearing a suit and tie.

The caption underneath read, "Metier attorney Edwin Beister."

Ethan whistled.

"I think we'd better pay Mister Transistor a visit," Ashley said. "He's still in the town jail, right?"

"Yeah," Ethan said. "But we can't go there tonight. It's too late. We'd only arouse suspicions."

"Okay," I said. "We'll do it tomorrow after school."

We shook on it three ways.

*　　　*　　　*

As I left the library, Ethan caught up with me. "I hope Ashley didn't get you down in there," he said. "She only acts that way because of what she's been through. I mean, she actually saw her own corpse."

"I'm fine," I said. "I'm just trying to decide which insult will sound best in Swahili."

Ethan laughed. Then his smile faded. "Listen," he said. "The creatures that tried to kill me and Ash, the one who's after you . . . they can make themselves look like anybody. Anybody at all. Like your mom, like Principal Lower, like Cleveland . . . even like Ashley and me."

I nodded.

"You can't trust anyone," Ethan continued. "And we can't communicate by regular means. It's too risky." He handed me a slip of paper. "This is a special phone number. Only Ashley and I know it. You can call it in an emergency."

"Sure," I said, stuffing the slip in my pocket. "I will."

But part of me was thinking, *How am I supposed to tell an emergency apart from everyday life?*

Ethan walked over to the bike stand and started unchaining a blue ten-speed. Somehow it was comforting to see that he still rode a bike, just like a regular kid. I'd half expected him to pull on a cape and fly home.

"Ethan?" I said, surprised to hear the tremor in my voice.

Ethan looked up at me. "Yeah?"

I finally asked the question that had been on my mind all evening: "What *are* we?"

Ethan merely shrugged. "I don't know," he said simply. "But I'm sure we'll find out, whatever the answer is." He walked his bike over to me, then placed his hand firmly on my shoulder. "And at least, right now, we're a team."

By the time I got home, my teeth were chattering from the cold. It was going to snow for sure. I slipped in beneath the garage door, being careful not to get wedged between the wall and the half-ton bar of chocolate. That would have made some headline: "Local Boy Crushed by Own Prize."

I brushed my teeth, said good night to Thad, who was still up reading, and slipped into bed.

"I'm not human," I whispered to myself, over and over in the dark. "I'm not human. . . . I'm not human. . . ."

It wasn't until the middle of the night that I realized I was also stark-raving mad.

I knew I was crazy because I was listening to a small, high-pitched voice, speaking from directly inside my mind. It was loud enough that it woke me up.

HUNGRY, it said. MUST GET FOOD.

Actually, come to think of it, I *was* a little hungry.

I suppose, if you're going to hear voices in your head, they might as well be accurate ones. I got up and headed to the kitchen.

COME QUICK, the voice said. FOOD! FOOD!

As I crept quietly down the stairs, the voice got louder. I noticed something odd: The voice didn't sound like just one person. It sounded like *millions*, all saying the same thing: GET FOOD NOW! MUST EAT! HUNGRY!

Weird, I thought, and shrugged. Apparently, this was some extrastrength grade of insanity.

Despite my plan to make a feast of the night's leftovers, once I arrived in the dark kitchen I walked right past the refrigerator. For some reason, I felt strangely compelled to keep going to the garage—as if I were being summoned.

I opened the garage door.

By now, the voices were deafening, incomprehensible. Yet they were calling to me, moving me forward. I couldn't stop my legs if I wanted to.

As I stepped into the garage, I clicked on the light switch.

The voices stopped just as suddenly as they had started.

Blinking in the fluorescent glare, I walked over to the half-ton bar of chocolate. Its foil wrapper almost seemed to radiate its own supernatural light.

Maybe that was what was calling me. Big things

sometimes have strange properties. The world's largest sapphire, weighing 9,719.5 carats, has a curse on it that's killed seventeen people and driven dozens more insane. Why not the world's largest chocolate bar?

But when I put my hand against the sugary behemoth, the voice came back again. This time it was panic-stricken:

GET AWAY! DANGER! ESCAPE!

I froze.

For a second, I was transported back to Mr. Holland's lab, where I'd heard a similar warning ring in my head.

That time, it was warning me about spiders.

This time, it was warning me about—

Ants.

About a dozen of them, crawling up my hand and along the arm that was leaning on the chocolate bar.

I recoiled in horror, and a piece of the foil wrapper pulled away, sticking to my hand. Underneath, revealed, the cocoa-brown surface of the chocolate bar was alive with even more ants. It swarmed with the little black insects—hundreds of them—that seemed disoriented at being uncovered.

I dropped the piece of foil in disgust and backed against the garage door, slapping myself, clawing my hair, trying to shake the tiny bugs off. My heart was going a million miles a minute. Of all the things I'd encountered that week, this was the most frightening.

Or at least I thought it was.

But turning to face the garage door, my racing heart stopped dead in my rib cage. I practically gagged in terror.

There was a face in the window, staring at me.

Chapter 13

"Jenny!" I said when I realized who it was. Suddenly, I was acutely aware that I was still in my pajamas. "I, uh, wish I'd known you were coming," I called through the glass. "I would have dressed."

"Keep your voice down," she said. She pointed toward our feet. "Can you open the garage door without waking anyone?"

"Sure, just a second," I said.

The icy wind hit me from under the garage door like a knife. I knew that the Wisconsin autumn was tropical compared with our record winter low of –24°F, but I was freezing. Jenny, on the other hand, didn't seem to mind.

"What are you doing out there?" I asked. A few flakes swirled into the garage.

"I have something important to tell you," she said.

"Don't you want to come in?" I asked. "You must be frozen solid."

"Oh," she said. "Sure." She stepped in under the garage door and lowered it behind her.

The moonlight illuminated her face from one side. Her eyes sparkled. Her face wasn't ruddy from the cold: It was smooth and beautiful. Her lips, on the other hand, were bright red, as red as—

Jenny Kim is in my house, after dark, all by herself, I suddenly realized, *and all I'm doing is staring at her.*

"Would you like something to eat?" I asked quickly, trying to think of what I might be able to get without waking up Mom or Thad. "We've got, uh . . . chocolate."

"No, thank you," she said politely. "I have an urgent message for you from Ethan and Ashley."

From Ethan and Ashley? Was Jenny in on our secret?

"What is it?" I asked.

"Ethan's dad, Chief Rogers, told him that Ed Beister's going to be moved to Madison for psychiatric evaluation in the morning," she said. "They're going to see him tonight and they want you with them."

"Tonight?" I asked. It was well after midnight.

Jenny nodded. "There's no time to lose," she said.

I squeezed into my snow boots and threw my ski jacket on over my flannels. I couldn't risk going upstairs to change: Mom might wake up, and she'd never let me out, no matter what lie I told her. Once my coat was fastened and my boots were laced, we headed into the bitterly cold night.

But as we stepped outside, I noticed something odd about Jenny. She genuinely wasn't feeling the cold. I mean, she was the supergirl of Metier Junior High and all, but she didn't even button her coat as she stepped outside.

Alarm bells were going off in my head.

How had Jenny gotten over here? She lived on the other side of town. Why would Ethan and Ashley send her and not come themselves? It didn't add up.

I looked deep into her pretty brown eyes. Was it possible that this vision of loveliness was actually . . . an alien? I was almost ready to go back to my first hypothesis: that I was losing my mind.

But I had to make sure.

"Uh, Jenny?" I said. "I think you're really neat, and pretty, and smart. . . ."

"Come on," Jenny said impatiently. "We can talk about that later. They're waiting for us."

"In fact," I went on, "I think the Korean expression that describes you best is *'nimon sangpanun donggayga gaywoongol dwaychomoggo do gaywoonyang dorobgoona.'*"

For those of you that aren't fluent in Korean, that translates into "Your face looks like something a dog barfed up, ate, and then barfed up again."

I held my breath. If I was lucky, the girl of my dreams was about to slap me across the face. If I wasn't . . . well, I didn't want to think about that.

For a second, Jenny's face was a complete blank.

Then she smiled.

"That's really sweet," she said. "But we have to get going."

My blood ran cold. Whoever this was, standing in front of me, it was *not* Jenny Kim.

"Just a minute," I said, trying not to stammer. "I need to get something."

Before she could protest, I dashed back into the house. Fumbling through the pockets of my ski jacket, I found the slip of paper Ethan had given me. If ever there was an emergency, this was it.

I grabbed the kitchen phone from the wall and dialed the number. *Please don't be busy*, I thought. *Please don't be busy*. I cast a nervous glance toward the garage.

It started to ring. I was in luck.

Or so I thought.

A moment later, the phone picked up on the other end.

"Hello, Ethan—" I began, but was immediately cut off by what sounded like a cross between a car alarm and a dentist's drill.

I recognized it instantly. It was a fax machine! Ethan must have left his fax machine connected to the phone. It could be a long time before he'd actually pick up— and time was one thing I didn't have.

114

I stood there for a few interminable seconds with the phone in my hand, wondering what I could do.

I was desperate. I knew Ethan was my last hope. Without his help, I was facing certain death.

Then, all of a sudden, my brain stopped hearing whistles and chirps. Instead, it heard *words:*

"Hello," the fax machine was saying. "Shake my hand? Hello? Shake my hand?"

"Yes," I said back to it, perfectly mimicking the fax noise. "Hello. I'll shake your hand."

I began relaying a message for Ethan. My voice came out in strange, garbled noises. I had become a piece of human office equipment.

But before I could finish the message, I saw a ghostly face at the kitchen window. It was Jenny, watching me. But the expression on her face was one I'd never seen Jenny wear. It was the expression of a cat looking at a mouse.

And then her whole face changed. It stretched and broadened, as if the bones in her skull were rearranging themselves, as if her skin were made of flesh-colored dough. Before I could react, she had transformed into a tall, thin man with a bulbous head and a sinister grin. Where her eyes had been . . . well, you know what was there.

The creature's arm punched right through the glass, seizing me around the neck. It squeezed—

And then everything went black.

_____ Chapter 14

I opened my eyes and immediately wished I hadn't.

I was in an old, dilapidated basement. Water dripped from the ceiling. The outdoor air, cold as ice, seemed to blow right in through the walls. And I was still in my pajamas. I was beginning to wish I'd let Mom buy me the superwarm thermal kind.

You could see the wiring in the ceiling above me. Pipes ran overhead like metal snakes. My hands were lashed behind my back to an old wooden support beam. I couldn't move.

I have to say this much for alien assassins: They know how to tie a knot.

I thought things couldn't get any worse, but I was wrong. After a moment, I heard heavy footsteps, and a strange, scraping noise, like a snowplow on asphalt. The noises got closer and closer until they were right outside the room.

Suddenly, the wooden door burst in. It was my bug-headed captor: That explained the heavy footsteps. But what about the scraping noise?

"I've brought you a friend," the alien sneered.

The creature dragged Ed Beister into the room. Ed's foil-covered parka scraped along as he moved, making a noise like a junk heap in motion. His hands were bound behind his back by several thick coils of rope. So were his ankles.

"Look who just escaped from jail," the alien bellowed, letting Ed's body clatter to the floor.

At first, I thought that the poor homeless man was dead. But after a moment, his head jerked, and he struggled to sit up. The alien laughed sadistically at his failed attempts.

I may not be the smartest kid in the world (that honor belongs to Omri Patel, a six-year-old East Indian with an IQ of 211), but it quickly dawned on me what Bug Head was planning on doing. After the scene Ed made in the Aliencounter arena, the police probably thought he was capable of anything. Including murder. The Bug was going to kill me and pin the crime on Ed.

Just as quickly, I saw the hole in his plan.

Ed was tied up and barely conscious! If they found him like that, they'd know it was a setup. Then they'd search for the real murderer. Eventually, they'd come across the alien spacecraft, and then they'd begin to build a defense. The planet would be saved. Unless—

The monster pulled a flat metal box from its hip pouch. It affixed the box to one of the decaying wooden support beams. "Time to die," the Bug boomed.

Unless it was planning on killing us both.

The alien punched a few codes into the strange box, which began humming ominously. "Thirty minutes," the creature said. "Time enough to reflect on the inferiority of your race before your life comes to an end." It laughed chillingly and started to leave the room.

With a furious motion, I turned myself around to face my captor. "*Kama matofali ni akili, wewe ni msikwao!*" I shouted.

The alien stopped dead in its tracks. "*What* did you say?" it asked.

"You heard me," I said.

The alien walked over to the box and punched in another code. "You will pay for your insolence. You now have ten minutes left on Earth." So saying, the alien turned, stepped over the body of Ed Beister, and left.

"What was that, kid?" the old man asked weakly, once the creature had gone. "Some kind of alien language?"

"No," I said. "Swahili. I told him that if brains were bricks, he'd be homeless."

Ed just stared at me.

"It wasn't my idea," I said.

"Can you get your hands free?" he asked.

"No," I said. "This rope is too tight. What about you? You're the one who just escaped from jail."

"I didn't escape," he replied. "That no-eyed freak came in pretending to be Chief Rogers. He tied me up and dragged me out. But in the morning, they're sure to think I broke out."

"In the morning, they're going to be cleaning us off the walls unless we think of something in a hurry," I replied.

"Maybe we can untie each other's hands," Ed said.

"It's worth a try," I said.

Ed wriggled across the floor toward me. I squirmed around until my hands were even with his. Quickly, we began to pry at the stubborn knots.

"You know, Ed," I grunted. "You don't really seem that crazy. I mean, you haven't screamed out 'Alien attack!' since you got here."

"I was never crazy," he said, biting his lip in concentration. "It's an act. I know too much. Pretending to be crazy is the only way I can be sure I'm safe."

"You call this safe?" I said. My fingers were burning as they pried at the rough fiber cords.

"This isn't working," Ed said, looking at the ropes binding my arms. "The knots are too tight. We're never going to loosen them in time."

I looked over at the metal box. It was humming more loudly now and radiating a weird energy.

The air around it seemed to quake and shimmer.

"How much time do you think we have left?" I asked.

"Five minutes," he said. "Not a second more."

Great, I thought. Just my luck to end my life at age thirteen in a cold, leaky basement. I'd never find out if Jenny liked me. I'd never find out about my father. And I'd never be able to warn my friends before the alien came for them.

Why had I been given such a useless superpower?

True, incredible fighting abilities or subaquatic talents wouldn't have helped me out of this one, either. But at least those sounded cool. What good was it to be able to speak to anyone when I was all alone?

No, I corrected myself. I wasn't quite alone. I was going to die with the town's only formerly crazy person. *And*, I noted sourly, looking at a pile of sawdust by the base of one of the wooden supports, *about ten million termites.*

I stared at the pile of sawdust a little longer. Termites. Which chew through wood. Termites, which, according to *The Guinness Book of Records*, have the strongest jaws, by pressure per square inch, of any animal. Which means they can—

DEVOUR.

The voice came, unbidden, into my head.

The same voice that I'd heard in Mr. Holland's lab. The same voice I'd heard in the garage. Telling me to escape. Warning me about the insects.

Wait a second. What if—

My mind raced.

What if the voices weren't *warning* me about the insects?

What if they were *coming* from the insects!

That's it!

I was "hearing" the communal voice of insects! *I can understand insect language*, I realized.

It suddenly made sense to me.

That's what was going on in the garage. Those ants had been lured by the scent of the chocolate— that's why they were all saying, "Food! Come here!" And when I suddenly entered the garage, I scared them away: "Danger! Escape!"

If I could understand them, I suddenly realized, I might be able to talk to them. I might be able to get them to help me.

But the thought made me shudder with every ounce of my being. Just the idea of termites—even *one* termite—made me feel faint.

There had to be another way out. Something else. *Anything* else.

Our situation wasn't that bad. It couldn't be.

"Two minutes remaining," Ed said. I realized he'd been slowly counting backward. "It was nice knowing you, kid."

It *was* that bad.

"Hold that thought," I said. "We're not dead yet."

Chapter 15

Feeling sick to my stomach, I squeezed my eyes shut and concentrated.

And there it was, in the back of my head, a little voice saying over and over again:

DEVOUR. DEVOUR.

Hungry, I tried to say back, to transmit from some inner part of my brain. *Very hungry. Hungry for . . . rope.*

I almost lost my lunch when I opened my eyes next. From every crack, crevice, and hole poked a chittering, black-eyed little head. I could almost hear their mandibles and antennae twitching, listening to me. I forced myself to go on.

Yes! I told them. *Must eat now! So hungry! Must eat! Delicious rope!*

They started to pour out onto the floor.

Each termite queen is capable of laying thirty

thousand eggs in an hour. With twenty-four hours in a day, that means more than half a million baby termites per queen per day.

The next sensation I felt was that entire half million, a solid river of twitching, spine-legged bugs, crawling up my body and over my arms.

I had found the answer to that timeless question: What's grosser than gross?

At that moment, the answer was "Me."

I looked over at Ed. He, too, was a solid mass of moving, pulsing termites. Then, suddenly, I couldn't see anything, as the bugs enveloped my head. I clenched my jaw tightly. If I could have opened my mouth, I would have screamed. But if I opened my mouth, I would have been breathing and eating bugs.

Then the cloud passed and a miracle happened: My hands were free. The rope was totally gone. Eaten away.

I scrambled to my feet. "How's our time?" I yelled to Ed.

"Twenty seconds," he shouted, already up and racing toward the cellar door. "Let's hit it, kid!"

I was right behind him.

Ed slammed into the door. The rotting wood splintered under his weight.

Thank you, I told the termites. *You saved my life*.

Then I ran out the door.

*　　*　　*

"Follow me," Mister Transistor shouted, running up a flight of crumbling stairs. We were still both covered in bugs. "This way!"

"How can you be sure?" I yelled.

"Because this is my home," he shouted back. "Or, it is for the next ten seconds, anyway!"

We dashed down a short corridor that ended in a heavy double door. We hit it at the same time, our bodies making a dull thud against the barricade. The doors swung open.

Then it was just like in the movies. We tumbled out into the snow. We staggered forward a few more steps as a high-pitched whine started to emanate from the cellar below. Before we had gone twenty feet, a violent explosion rocked the building to its foundation. Chunks of concrete and wood sailed through the air all around us.

The force of the explosion lifted me off my feet and threw me, face forward, into a snowbank. I got the wind knocked out of me, but that seemed to be the extent of the damage.

I listened for any desperate termite screams, but there weren't any. They were gone, I realized. Then, as I watched, the roof of the old wooden house collapsed inward, sending a shower of sparks into the night sky, like a blizzard of fireflies.

I looked over at Ed. A few minutes ago, I only *thought* he was homeless. Now I knew he was.

"Are you okay?" I said.

"I'm fine," he replied.

"But your house!" I said.

"It's not important," he said, grinning a two-toothed smile. He shook the snow from his beard. "I still have my space antenna."

Great. The explosion had knocked him back into Looney Land. "Your space antenna?" I asked skeptically.

"Follow me," Ed said.

Snow swirled gently to the ground. To the east, the sky was a faint pink where the sun began to peek over the horizon. It wasn't bitterly cold anymore. The air had that gentle warmth you get after a heavy snow.

I don't know what I expected to see when we got to the "space antenna." Maybe a car antenna mounted on a tree. Or a big stick wrapped in aluminum foil. Or maybe just the world's largest collection of tin cans.

We traipsed through the snow-blanketed woods for close to twenty minutes. The path we followed wound from side to side through the trees and in several places crossed back over itself.

Clearly, Ed wasn't taking any chances tipping off the aliens to his location. He walked with an unerring sense of direction, making sharp turns and crouching under overhanging branches as if on instinct. I'd have bet he could have done it blindfolded. And I'd have bet he trained himself for just such a possibility.

"We're here," Ed said, shouldering away some late-growth bushes. "Look."

My eyes followed his outstretched arm. And then the breath caught in my mouth.

There, in the clearing ahead, was an enormous radio tower, a cross-lattice of iron bars stretching right to the top of the tree line, like a thin Eiffel Tower.

Even in the dim light of dawn, I could see that the sides had been buffed and polished to a high sheen. An intricate webbing of wire and metal, like a ten-story cat's cradle, wound through the hollow of the tower. It reminded me of the metal crosshatching on the sides of the world's largest radio antennae, the Very Large Array outside Santa Fe, New Mexico.

"It's beautiful," I said, too astonished to think very clearly.

"I've been working on it for nearly ten years," Ed said. "Ever since I started monitoring their transmissions."

"They?" I asked. "You mean you can actually receive the aliens' radio signals?"

But I was interrupted by a sudden noise. A crashing in the woods nearby.

Instantly, I dropped to one leg and spun in the direction of the sound. *Either I'm getting good at this*, I thought, *or all that laser tag is really paying off.*

There was no way we could escape in the thick snow. Ed grabbed a tree branch off the ground. Other than that, we were totally unarmed. I cursed myself for having let the aliens follow us. What I wouldn't have given for a torque blaster! I guessed we were going to have to rely on my raw cunning and skill.

And in that case, we were dead.

But as I caught my first glimpse of the creature that emerged from the tree line, I heaved a sigh of relief. Dark brown bangs, black eye shadow, black rubber bracelets peeking out from the sleeves of her black-hooded ski parka: It was Ashley, all right. Was it my imagination, or did she actually look kind of pretty in the early morning light?

"Hey!" she cried. "I'm so glad you're all right!"

"Keep your voice down," I said gruffly. Secretly, I was pleased that she cared. But the less she knew about that, the better.

"Hey, Jack," said a familiar voice in an X-Men jacket. "I got your note." Ethan waved a piece of fax paper at me. In strange, blurry letters, it read, "Ethan. This is Jack. Help me. Jenny is—" That's where the words ended.

Not half bad for a first timer, I thought.

"We had no idea where you'd been taken," Ethan

said. "First we called Jenny's home, but her grandma told us she was sound asleep." He smirked. "Boy, did grandma get mad when we told her to wake Jenny up. But she did it."

"Jenny had no idea where you were, either," Ashley continued, "so we headed to your house. We saw the broken glass on the ground and figured you'd been captured . . . or worse. Then we heard the explosion."

"*Ashley* heard it," Ethan clarified. "I *saw* it. We went to explore the wreckage, then followed your trail here."

Ethan's eyes flickered to the figure at my side. "Ed Beister?" he asked, sounding surprised.

"The same," Ed said, giving a little bow.

"Ed saved my life," I said.

"And *he* saved mine," Ed announced. He gestured at me, practically braining Ashley with the branch still clenched in his fist. "Sorry," he said, tossing the tree limb to the ground. "We thought you two might be that alien coming back to finish the job."

"For now they probably think that both of you were killed in that bomb blast," Ethan said. "But sooner or later, they'll realize you weren't."

"Ethan's right," Ashley said. "We aren't safe. They'll be back."

"Well, when they do," I said, "we'll be waiting for them. And we'll make them sorry they ever left home."

We shook on it, a three-way shake.

As if on cue, the ground began to hum. A weird, high-pitched wail rang in my ears, growing in intensity. It sounded like a siren going off.

"A transmission," Ed said. "They're sending a transmission. Quick—I have to transcribe what they're saying."

Ed grabbed a thick leather-bound notebook and a set of earphones from a hiding place on the underside of the antenna. The earphones were connected by a thick copper cable to the base of the tower. Ed got a pen out, prepared to write.

"Can you actually understand what they're saying?" I asked.

"No," Ed replied. "All I can do is record the sounds and how often they make them."

"Do you mind if I try?" I asked.

"Not at all," Ed said. "Go right ahead."

"Jack," Ashley asked. "Do you think you can actually do this?"

"So far today, I've talked in Swahili, termite, and fax," I said. "I'm ready to try alien."

I put the headphones on my head and closed my eyes to concentrate.

The sound of the alien transmission was a horrible, staticky rhythm. Occasionally, there was a squeal of feedback that almost blew the headphones off my head. But after a few moments, words began to form against the back of my brain: black letters swirling together, fitting into place. Then I saw the whole message in front of me. And my blood ran cold.

Begin transmission, the message read.

TARGET: JACK RAYNES.
LOCATION: METIER, WISCONSIN.
ORDERS: SEEK AND DESTROY.
STATUS: FATAL HIT.
MISSION COMPLETED.

How long would it be before the aliens realized I was still alive? How long would it be before they came back for round two? I looked at my two new best friends, remembering the words I'd spoken so confidently a moment ago: "When they come back, we'll be waiting for them."

If they weren't already here.

About the Author

Chris Archer grew up in New Jersey, where he spent most of his childhood wishing he had special powers.

He now divides his time between New York City and Los Angeles, California. When Chris is not writing books and screenplays, he enjoys going to scary movies, playing piano (badly), and reading suspense novels.

He has never been to Wisconsin.

What would you do
if you saw an alien…
in the mirror?

For Ethan Rogers, Ashley Rose and Jack Raynes of
Metier, Wisconsin, turning thirteen means much more
than becoming a teenager. It means discovering they
have amazing alien powers. Ethan is a skilled fighter–the
ultimate warrior. Ashley can stay under water as long as
she wants. Jack can speak and understand any language–
human and otherwise.

They don't know why it happened, but someone
does…and that someone or something wants them
dead.

MINDWARP #1: ALIEN TERROR

MINDWARP #2: ALIEN BLOOD

MINDWARP #3: ALIEN SCREAM

By Chris Archer

And look for more mindwarp novels, coming in 1998.

 A MINSTREL® BOOK

Published by Pocket Books

1429-01